Cadence

by

Claire Davon

Lyrical Interludes, Book Three

Cadence

Cover Art by *Kristian Norris*

The Wild Rose Press, Inc.
PO Box 708
Adams Basin, NY 14410-0708
Visit us at www.thewildrosepress.com

Publishing History
First Edition, 2024
Trade Paperback ISBN 978-1-5092-5682-2
Digital ISBN 978-1-5092-5683-9

Lyrical Interludes, Book Three
Published in the United States of America

Acknowledgements

After the books that became *Reprise* and *Overture* were finished, Jessica Baker and Kai Halara's stories were begging to be told. Like *Overture*, the first version of *Cadence* (at the time the book had no title) was written over a decade ago and has done many transformations since then. As the industry changed, so did this story. I am over the moon about the way it turned out and hope that you are too.

Thanks, as always, go to Josette, my editor. She taught me about expletive constructions and fixes all my bad habits!

Special call out to all who are following the Lyrical Interludes journey. You're the best!

Chapter One

As a musician, Jess understood timing.

She was about to be late.

She ran across the parking structure to the elevator, checking her phone as she did so. She'd missed a call from Ally Wilson telling her the executives were in the conference room, waiting for her.

Jess would admit to nobody but herself that the recent advisor, Kai Halara, was why she'd taken extra care with her hair and makeup. She'd met him for the first time two weeks ago when he sat in on a strategy meeting for her upcoming tour. She hadn't been that thunderstruck by a man in a long time.

She was aware of the fragility of her position. Despite all her hopes, Jess' album numbers were flat, the reception to her songs indifferent. Not what she had dreamed about as a preteen. Then she had imagined herself on talk shows and late night, plugging her album and charming the masses.

Reality, as that darned thing was so often, was different.

Ally's assistant was pacing by the door when Jess plunged through the double-paned glass. She gestured to Jess and indicated the hallway. "They're waiting."

Jess forced herself to slow to a walk. She couldn't arrive at the meeting disheveled and out of breath. She smoothed her blonde locks and wished she had a mirror to check her appearance. She settled for the brief images in the framed posters as she went past. She prayed none of her emotions showed on her face.

She hoped.

Gordon, the label head, was glowering when she walked into the conference room. "You're late."

She stuffed down a flare of guilt and managed to meet his fierce stare. "Last-minute stuff came up. I'm here now."

When Jess entered, her gaze went to Kai like a moth to a flame, and she barely registered the rest of the occupants of the room. His hair was shoulder length and straight, the color matching his dark eyes—the ones that went right through her. He had judged her, and her music, and found her lacking. She was sure of it.

"She's not late, Gordon." Ally's voice was just this side of impatient.

"We've got no time to waste. We should have gotten started already." Gordon's terse tone matched Ally's.

Through it, Kai watched, saying nothing.

"I'm sorry." Jess couldn't afford to get a reputation as being difficult this early in her career. Kai was at the center of her confusion, and that couldn't continue.

"It's fine." Ally's voice was clipped. "We don't need to do much for the Ryder Bingham tour. It's a handful of dates in Northern California and Nevada. This could have been handled over video conferencing."

Gordon shook his head. "I wanted the personal touch."

Jess didn't see why, but that wasn't her call to make. "You got it. I'm happy to do whatever is needed."

She had done research into Kai over the past two weeks. He was thirty-five and, near as she could tell, not married. She had been unable to find out if he had a girlfriend. Not that she'd been scouring the internet for that.

His hard rock label, Apposite, had failed in the recent past, leaving him unemployed. How that made him a judge of country music, she wasn't sure, leading her to suspect that Kai was here for different reasons besides the nebulous "tour manager" title Gordon had thrown around. Jess had learned long ago to hope for the best and prepare for the worst. Gordon wouldn't have given in to her not-so-subtle suggestion that Kai come onto her tour if it didn't suit him. Something more was brewing. Kai might have been brought on to take stock of Jessica Baker and figure out what Shatter Sound should do with her.

If she was right—and Jess was pretty confident of her conclusions—her future was in Kai's hands. His big, capable hands…

Kai nodded at something the head of marketing, Dirk Roberts, was saying before focusing on Jess. His pupils were so dark that she couldn't find any light in them. In addition, the stony set to his face gave nothing away.

When she discovered Ryder had pushed for her to open this leg of his tour, she'd wondered if he was going to suggest resurrecting their fling. A quick series of phone calls dispelled that notion, and Jess was grateful for that. She'd have been forced to choose and would have hated that choice. Ryder never reached out to her after that single night in Austin, but men could be strange. Their conversations had contained nothing but business, and she relaxed before she got excited. This tour would help her sputtering career. She was relieved she didn't have to say no, because of Ryder or Kai. Men came and went, but the ability to take care of herself was all-important.

Jess' cheeks heated when she dared check Kai out. His arms remained folded, but he inclined his head to her.

"Right. Let's do this," Gordon said.

Jess focused her attention on him, trying to erase the impact of Kai from her mind. "I came, as requested. I thought everything was, for the most part, wrapped up. Is there something wrong with the tour?"

Gordon didn't look at her—also not a good sign. "No. I had to go over some final details with you and ask Kai if he had any questions."

Jess dodged Kai's scrutiny. She was twenty-five, not twelve. She was a woman who had grown up too fast and understood what the opposite sex was about. Even if he hadn't been there to take away her livelihood, he was not for her. Men like Kai Halara had serious lives and girlfriends that did important things like save the whales and march on government buildings, not ones who wrote and sang songs for a living.

When Jess went to the conference table, she sat next to Ally, turning away from Kai.

Then all ideas of men with agendas faded as they began to discuss the tour. Kai watched the proceedings with apparent detachment. If she hadn't been attracted to him, his distant, supercilious attitude would have grated. Somehow, because the person was Kai, the haughtiness made him more interesting.

Then again, that was her style—courtesy of a shitty childhood. Disconnected parents created lifelong trauma, and despite her sessions with a therapist, Jess was pretty sure she had not put aside her upbringing.

Not that a guy like Kai would care about that.

****

Kai's first sight of Jessica had hit him like a freight train.

He watched her as she focused on each speaker. Her manager should have been there but, for whatever reason, either hadn't been invited to this particular meeting or hadn't shown. Her questions showed that she'd done her research and wasn't relying on those around her to advise the correct steps.

That much poise in a woman twenty-five years old was remarkable. The haunted maturity in her didn't match the shining blonde hair and full lips. He didn't go for blondes as a matter of preference—or women as young as Jessica. Though some might not think so, ten years was a big difference.

"Will the fans be expecting CDs at the merch table? Or is it a waste of time? In the past, artists would sign them at their table after the show, but all the teens download stuff, not buy physical copies." Gordon focused on Kai.

He started to answer when Dirk cut in.

"It's never a bad idea to have bespoke merchandise. The buyers for that will skew older, but we might draw in some who are younger. We've got T-shirts, stickers, and koozies. Those are what I have found move the needle more than the music. Though CDs are faded in popularity, some still want them. If we had more money, I would have done something in a limited edition but didn't have the funds."

"What do *you* think, Kai?" Gordon's voice echoed across the conference table, almost as a challenge.

Country was a form of music Kai wasn't that familiar with. Apposite had been a rock label, specializing in hard rock and speed metal. Apposite. His failed venture. It had been a long shot when he started it, but he had always been persistent and assumed he could tough it out and make the endeavor a success in time.

In that, he'd been wrong.

He cleared his throat, surprised that Gordon had addressed him. Kai studied Jess' picture on the back of the CD. The picture wasn't like the real-life woman. This was every bit a professional portrait, with her hair teased out and blown straight, the wind lifting it just back from her face. She had a white dress on, creating a sexy yet virginal effect.

The real Jessica Baker had her own raw sensuality that called to him in a way he had no business entertaining.

"I am with Dirk. She can sign the liner notes on the physical copies. We will have postcards and download cards for those who buy it online. Dirk's got the right idea for merch. Patches are good too, if you are still searching for suggestions. Those should cover our bases."

Gordon nodded and started speaking to Dirk in low tones.

Studying the real-life woman in front of the conference table, Kai decided he liked her better today than in the glamour shot on the CD. Her hair had a natural wave to it and curled down her back. She had more makeup on than he was expecting, with a smoky liner around her lids and mascara. Her peasant blouse was in a muted green that complemented her skin, jeans and cowboy boots completing the outfit.

"Kai?"

He focused on Ally Wilson with the CD still in his hand. "Yes?"

"Did you have any input on the set list? We're going to end with 'Susan the Magician,' of course, since that's the first release, but any opinions about the rest?"

He reviewed what they had said about the song choices, though he hadn't been giving it his full concentration. "I would move the third song to be second so you've got a break between tempos, but it's a short set, so it won't make that much of a difference either way."

"Great. Thanks. I'll talk to her manager. Appreciate the input. Jess, will you sign the CDs?"

If it wasn't his imagination, Jessica's attention flicked to him before landing on Ally. Kai struggled to keep his face neutral.

"Of course I will. Give me all you have. And a pen."

The meeting broke, and Kai wondered why Gordon had forced all of them to attend this thing in person. Perhaps the label president meant it as a flex to show his power.

Ally lingered as the rest filed out of the conference room, leaving Kai and Jess behind. Those folks had offices, but Kai did not. He worked from home, making this even stranger. The entire thing had been unnecessary.

He approached Jess as she signed. He resisted the urge to turn on his heel and walk away when she raised her head to acknowledge him. No matter his reason, she would take it a different way.

You should have kept your distance.

Too late now.

"Hi, Kai," she said.

"Jess." He made his spine straight and crossed his arms again. "Good move on the physical copies. These will work for giveaways."

Her skin had a luminous quality that reminded him again how pretty she was.

"Of course. Let me sign one for you. Unless you don't do CDs?"

"I tend to keep an uncluttered house, but I'll take one. I've listened to your songs on streaming, but a CD isn't a bad idea."

A smile tugged at the corners of her mouth. Kai wouldn't make the arrogant assumption that it had anything to do with what he said. Jess could be thinking about things she had to do once she was out of the meeting.

She handed the CD back to him, and their fingers brushed. She shuddered almost imperceptibly. The slight tell matched the burning awareness soaring through his body.

He focused on what she had written over the liner notes. "To Kai Halara," he read, a frown developing. "Thanks for being in my corner."

Irony wasn't a quality he'd expected in Jessica, but when he met her gaze, something old and far too wise lurked behind the pretty exterior. In that searing instant, she appeared much older than twenty-five.

Ally caught her attention and motioned to the front of the room. Jess shifted her focus to Ally. The prickles on his skin faded, making him mourn the loss of contact.

"Well," Jess said, rubbing her hands on her jeans and rising, "I've got work to do. Bye, Kai. We'll be in each other's company more than you care to be in no time."

"I am eager to begin our association."

"Anything else you need before I head off?" She stood a short distance away, her hair forming a halo around her.

His fingers flexed with the urge to touch the strands—and her. He took a step back to quell the urge. "None at this time. You're aware for this tour to have its desired impact you'll have to make the most of your brief time onstage."

"Of course. That's my intention. I never shortchange my fans. I just wish I had more of them."

Ally approached the table again. She might not be Terri August, the woman who had been his right hand and second-in-command until Apposite failed, but was no slouch. He'd determined not to get close to any of the Shatter Sound employees, but despite that, he liked this no-nonsense woman. The fact that Ally and Terri were friends spoke well of her. Contacts were a lifeblood in this business. He had already reached out and was tracking down more information about a possible opening at Plausive Records. So far, the rumors were just that, but Kai was a patient man.

In most things.

"Good. This will be a fluid process. I might have more changes to recommend, depending on the reception we get. If you're going to go for the top, you've got to aim high. That's the best way to succeed." He waited for her to make the obvious statement—that his label had failed and he was in no position to pass judgment. He wasn't sure if he was surprised or satisfied when she said nothing.

Ally shook her head. "Kai, I'm counting on you. We

need this tour to give her a boost. You've got the experience to figure out what to change. I'm open to any suggestions. We can make changes on the fly since I'll be joining you until Vegas."

Gordon's voice boomed out from the doorway. Kai hadn't noticed he'd come back.

"He'll do his job. That's why I'm paying this guy the big bucks. Ally, a word."

"Sure thing, Gordon. Thanks, Kai. Terri says great things about you, and I can't wait to get all of them into action." With that she retreated, taking the CDs with her.

When Ally was gone, Kai nodded to Jess. "We should discuss the tour. Are you free for dinner tomorrow?"

Her brows knitted, lining her gorgeous face as the singer gazed at him in confusion. "I don't have plans. Besides food. Everyone has to eat."

He could have drowned in the depths of her big brown eyes.

"Let me take you out so that we can continue this conversation. I'll come for you at seven. I will get your address from Ally."

"All right. Until then."

Gordon came back to the conference room as Jess exited, and focused on Kai. "What do you think?"

Kai had no intention of revealing to anyone what was rolling around in his brain. Perceived weakness was blood in the water to a shark like Gordon.

"Hard to say. My expertise is in rock music, but a good hook is universal, and she has those. The country market is saturated with solo artists, but she has talent. With time and some luck, she has a chance."

Gordon's attention went to the open door before he

leaned in and lowered his voice until Kai alone could hear his words. "I'm thinking of dropping her. Time isn't a friend to new labels. We need results, now, and Jess hasn't been providing them. As I said earlier, your mission on this tour is to find out if I've got anything to salvage or need to just cut my losses. Clear?"

Kai had a million things he could say. In his former company, he'd kept bands on longer than had been wise. Sometimes it paid off, until it did not. The proof of that was in the failed venture and a catalog that belonged to someone else now.

He was in no position to give advice, and his job wasn't to argue with the man who'd brought him on for a specific reason. Kai gave Gordon a brisk nod, showing none of his emotions behind his blank exterior. "Got it."

Chapter Two

Jess stared at the dresses heaped on her bed in front of her. Kai's words echoed in her mind, resounding with a greater meaning than the man had intended.

"Are you free for dinner tomorrow?"

His invitation had been delivered with no trace of emotion on his face. She was unclear why he had suggested it. He didn't need to get a meal with her to help her with the tour. If he were anyone besides Kai, she might have expected he was angling for a hookup.

She'd texted him later and advised that he shouldn't be obligated to keep their plans. His response was swift.

—I must give Shatter Sound their money's worth. In order to do that, I will have to understand your ins and outs so I can determine what I should focus my attention on.—

Though she considered arguing that she didn't need fixing, numbers didn't lie. Her record wasn't the smash hit she'd imagined all her life. Since she started playing guitar, when her one listener was her much older brother Rocky, she'd dreamed of her songs being number one on the charts.

The truth had been a letdown. Her album was struggling, and her future was at risk. She needed all the help she could get. If that meant dealing with a man who was impossible to read, so be it. He might be able to propel her up the tough ladder of the thousands of artists trying to make it. He might be there to axe her from the label, but perhaps she could turn that to her advantage. If she impressed Kai, she stood a chance of staying.

Jess held up a blue shirtwaist dress that had a front button placket in a matching color, before tossing it on the pile of discards. *Too much like a mom.* It had been a gift from her parents, one of the few Christmas presents she'd received. She was lucky the dress was the right size.

She checked the hangers in her closet in case she'd missed an item hanging in the back.

That's what she got for living in jeans, short tops, and cowboy boots. In the world of country music, her attire was fine, but it didn't work for lunch with dour former label owners.

The blare of the television was audible through her open bedroom door. Whistles and low announcer voices told her a game of some sort was on. Michelle, her roommate, was a sports nut, and though they made strange roommates, the arrangement worked.

Jess snatched two of the best off the mattress and padded into the living room. Michelle acknowledged her with a nod and paused the TV.

"Help. I can't make a decision." Holding a butter-yellow maxi dress in front of her, Jess let her friend check it out and then pulled the second one in front of her. This one was a blue paisley-print short-sleeved dress that fell just to her knees.

"The blue one," Michelle said. "The yellow washes your coloring out." She turned her attention back to the game as Jess hurried back into her bedroom to change.

A quick glance at the clock told her she had fifteen minutes until Kai arrived. She was adding silver hoop earrings to her ears to go with the bangle bracelet and chunky necklace she'd already donned, when the doorbell rang. She glanced at her phone, which showed the time as right before seven.

Somehow, that wasn't a surprise.

Jess buzzed Kai in and gave him directions to their apartment. She waited with the front door open until the elevator dinged and his footsteps echoed in the hallway. Then she poked her head out to gesture him to their place.

Dressed in a black silk shirt buttoned to the collar and matching sport coat and slacks, Kai resembled a sleek panther—if cats wore glasses. The frameless lenses made his cheekbones stand out on his face.

"You're early," she said when he entered.

He consulted his watch and showed it to her. The large dial had the words *Apposite Records* across it and a stylized lightning bolt logo. "Not according to this." His hair was brushed and tied back with a leather thong, emphasizing the strong planes of his face. A rich, masculine scent clung to him.

She pointed to the fifties-diner-style wall clock in the middle of the dining room. "This says you're five minutes ahead of schedule."

He took out his phone from the black messenger bag slung over his shoulder and checked the display. Without speaking, he bowed, acceding the point. "I'm Kai Halara." He raised a hand to the woman in the living room.

"Michelle." Her roommate didn't move from the sofa but waved a hand his direction.

Jess fastened the ankle straps of her low-heeled pumps and nodded to him. "Ready."

He glanced at the wall clock and back at her. "Perfect timing."

Michelle bobbed her head at their goodbyes. Whistles and the sound of the ball slapping on the court floor filled the room as Jess closed and locked the door. Her hands were sweating, but she didn't dare rub them on her nice dress to ruin it. This would have been so much easier if she'd worn jeans. She should have.

Kai gestured to a black hybrid SUV parked outside the gate to their complex. He helped her into the car, lifting her so she could slide her legs onto the seat. The contact of his strong fingers and forearms made her skin tingle.

"I didn't realize you had a roommate." He started the engine and merged into traffic. "I was under the impression you lived alone."

She began to snort in amusement before turning the sound into a scoff. "On Cahuenga? In Hollywood? I could never afford it without assistance. You of all people understand how little an artist makes—if anything—off their first album. Michelle and I have been roommates for three years. I'm gone a lot of the time, so she has the run of the place. She watches my stuff and starts my car if I'm away for an extended period. It gives me somewhere to go when I'm in town, and it's located near to the things I need. If I ever got to play the Hollywood Bowl, I could walk to it."

"If you were big enough to play the Bowl, you wouldn't have to." He gave her a quick glance, and if she wasn't mistaken, his gaze held approval. "This dress is pretty on you. I haven't seen you in anything besides jeans."

She sorted through several responses in her head.

She considered asking why he had invited her to dinner but couldn't risk the answer.

This entire night, and his presence on the tour, could help her career if she was smart. She had to remember that. "Thanks. Where are we going?"

"My friends recommended a new fusion restaurant on Melrose. Is that all right, or would you prefer something different? I should have asked first."

Jess recalled all the times she'd had to fend for herself in the leftovers in the pantry or whatever Rocky had brought the last time he visited. Often dinner had been cereal—if the milk was still good. Sometimes, she ate the forgotten can of sardines or canned meat, way in the back of the cabinet, that tasted like metal. On occasion, her meal was out of the dumpster behind the grocery store near them. Amazing, what got thrown away. The money that might have gone for food was spent on liquor. The alcohol killed their appetite, and their preteen daughter didn't matter.

Jess shook herself to shed the images. That was the past, and the delicious Kai was here. She needed to stay focused on the present. "That's fine. I can always find something to eat, even at vegan restaurants." She'd bet he was a vegetarian.

"Good. Thank you for being flexible."

They made slow progress from her apartment building down Cahuenga. They were in the middle of the Hollywood Hills, and traffic was dense.

"I think you will enjoy this restaurant. The reviews are good." Kai started to say something more but then closed his mouth.

She'd give anything to be told what he'd been about to say.

Kai turned right onto Melrose before driving the rest of the distance down the crowded street without speaking. He handed his keys to the valet before moving to her side to help hand her out.

As an up-and-coming artist, Jess had had her share of fans and those attracted to her slice of fame. She'd been fawned over, but the experience was different with Kai. He was danger wrapped up in a taut body and gorgeous hair.

The place was packed, the buzz of conversation all around them. Kai gave his name to the host, greeting the man with a tilt of his head and slight bow.

"Do you always do that?" she whispered.

"Do what?"

"Act like you're in a dojo when you greet someone." She approximated his movements as best she could.

He let out a chuckle and shook his head.

If he was stunning when he was solemn, he was spectacular when amused, the cheerfulness lighting up his face and stripping years away.

"Interesting observation." One hand moved to touch her, but he stopped. "My martial arts training is a significant part of my life. I suppose some of that has filtered down to my everyday activities. I'm also half Japanese."

"What's the rest? Where are you from?"

"Greek. I grew up in Hawaii. Come. He's seating us."

As they were seated, Kai placed her in the chair facing away from the outside door before sliding into the one opposite.

Her brother had always chosen that seat, saying something about being in a better position to defend her if trouble came. She'd always loved when Rocky said that—the words made her imagine she was cared for.

Perhaps Kai wasn't as modern a man as his messenger bag and trendy glasses suggested.

He lifted the wine menu in a silent question. Jess hesitated and then nodded. He selected a wine that the waiter informed them was one of their most popular.

After the waiter left, Kai tapped the table. "The online reviews raved about the salmon, but they have many choices."

She used her phone to access the QR code on the surface, then scrolled through the selections. The faint whiff of an earthy cologne clung to him. She didn't recall him wearing cologne in their prior meetings. The care in that action suggested that this was a date, but this night wasn't about men and women. About dating.

Even if she wished that she could use the word— and the evening—in association with the dark-haired man.

"Noted. Thanks." She wouldn't mention she didn't like salmon. Or fish in general. "Perhaps one of the pasta dishes—although I can't eat that often and stay tour ready."

He gave her a quick smile that she could have basked in for days. The waiter brought the bottle and poured a little in Kai's glass for him to taste it. She watched as the red swirled around before he put the glass to his lips.

She never wished to be a glass so much in her life.

After they ordered, Kai poured some wine for her. His square-cut nails and calluses suggested he did many things for himself. She'd love to know what those were.

"I'm sorry. I didn't ask if you favored red or white."

He paused with his hand on the glass. "I can get something else."

She would not take his attentiveness to heart. That would be dumb. "Red is fine. I don't drink much as a general rule, so it doesn't matter. Shouldn't we get white if we're going to order fish?"

"I don't listen to pairings. They are there to sell wine and nothing more."

Jess wished she had the gift of gab but left that to the slick PR guys. "You said your friends recommended this place. Who?"

When he didn't answer right away, she wondered if she'd overstepped. He took a sip and set the glass down. He blotted his lips with the napkin before laying it back in his lap.

Glass. Napkin. She would love to be either one at this time.

"Clarke Masters, the former singer of Attraction, is a good friend of mine, as is his fiancée, Terri. They told me that this would live up to my standards." His smile was rueful and took years off his age. "They think I'm too wound up. They were right—about the location and me."

She absorbed the words, taking a sip of her wine without tasting the alcohol. She took a second, longer drink and then set the glass down. "I don't know either person, though of course I've heard of Clarke. He's outside my time, but Rocky liked his music, so I have some of Attraction's tunes on my playlist. Ally has mentioned Terri. I think they're friends."

The waiter laid down a bed of microgreens with a vinaigrette on the side and retreated.

"What about you, Jessica? Who can you call friend?

Are you and your high school and college pals connected on social media? Or do you leave that to the press and keep your friends out of sight—like your roommate?"

Panic pierced her as she struggled for ways to answer the question. She could come up with nothing he would understand. "I don't have any from my childhood, so that is not an issue on social media. As far as current day—I've got enough. You met Michelle. There's Craig and Ally. Others too, but they come and go. That's the business for you. None from my past. I couldn't name more than five from high school."

To cover her words, Jess took a sip of the wine. She didn't often drink, and the sensation was a buzz under her skin. Jess picked up her fork and pierced a piece of the greenery while avoiding Kai's scrutiny.

It might have been an eon before he spoke. "Craig?"

She bit her lip with a quick, nervous motion, wishing she'd not been so forthcoming. "Old boyfriend. He is a friend of Ally's, and he was the one who brought me to her attention. We, well, we didn't work out, but we stayed friends."

"That's interesting." His words were clipped, their syllables sharp. Though the light was dim in the restaurant's interior, she noted that his jaw tightened.

She wouldn't ask the next question.

Yes, she would.

"And you? Do you have a girlfriend? Or boyfriend?"

The curve of his lips might have been a smile. "Nobody special. I spent most of the last year trying to keep my label going. I had little time for relationships. Now I have time, but this is Los Angeles. Few women will associate with a failed executive."

Or a failing artist. The ramifications of the month on tour, and what that could mean for her future, raced through her.

Jess picked at her salad. He'd said women, so he was straight or at least bi. She had a chance…she had to stop.

He cleared his throat, and she forced herself to meet his gaze.

"Never mind my social life. Regarding your online presence, we should check into how we can work that to your advantage. I imagine you've got all manner of friends. You have a natural friendliness and had to be one of the most popular kids in school."

A stab of irrational pique pierced Jess that he was fooled by her social media. "You'd be surprised. You've heard the saying, I'm sure. On the internet, nobody knows you're a dog. Why did you ask me to come out tonight? We could have done this over email or text."

The desire and longing playing over his face shook her with its strength. Then the image was gone, replaced by a faint, detached grin.

"If we're going to work and tour together, we need to make the most of this time. If not, my expertise—the whole reason Shatter Sound brought me on—is wasted."

Everything he didn't say—and she suspected—lay between the syllables.

"Got it. Project Jessica Baker has commenced. That's what they're paying you for."

It might have been her imagination, but a flicker of disapproval crept over Kai's face, and his gaze shuttered.

Before he could respond, their entrées came.

"Good. Then we're on the same page."

She fixed on her dish, her appetite fleeing. He might have been sitting in front of her, but he was a million miles away. Strands of his dark hair escaped the tie as he dug into his entrée.

If she was going to make the most of this, she needed to stay focused. No man, no matter how gorgeous, should interfere with that.

Her future, and his, might depend on her overcoming this latest obstacle.

Chapter Three

Taking her to dinner had been a mistake. Kai wondered why he had put himself in this situation. Jessica had to be aware of her beauty and ability to charm those around her. That combination always made artists difficult to manage. She wasn't for him, despite what his body was telling him. He had an unpleasant job to do and couldn't allow sentiment to get in his way.

She gazed at him as they drove. The knot in his stomach tightened.

"What's next? Now that you've assessed the 'real' Jessica Baker."

I have so much more to learn. "I'll put together an action plan and email it to you and your manager. I've got some ideas but need to do some outreach before committing. Country music is not my area."

She took a breath but said nothing. Prickles of discomfort moved along his skin. Awareness buzzed under his collar. Kai pushed back the sensation. Jess should date an artist or an athlete—someone powerful to raise her profile. Not a temp with a terrible track record.

He would keep his distance. For both their sakes.

What the hell had tonight been about?

He would not answer his inner saboteur. That guy was a jerk. Jessica inhaled but, again, didn't speak.

The silence was interminable. Even for a man who enjoyed the quiet, Kai's nerves were dancing on edge.

"You were going to say something?"

Her blonde hair was dappled in light and shadow as they drove through the dense streets to her apartment. "My manager is working on the same thing. That's what he's there for."

"You've got Dirk and Ally too, and Shatter Sound. I'm a part of that. We're all trying to do our jobs." He wondered if she was aware what Gordon was up to. Jessica Baker was savvy—she had to understand her deal with Shatter Sound was in jeopardy.

"Of course. I'd appreciate your input." She put her hand on the console, so near his thigh that he swallowed.

When he cast his mind back over dinner, he realized that while he'd had less than a full glass of wine, the bottle had been empty when they left the restaurant. That meant that she'd had most of it. That explained her slight unsteadiness and the softness around her jawline.

She was drunk.

"I'll provide everything I can. What you choose to do with my suggestions is up to you. It is up to each individual to find their own path. I never force someone to do something that goes counter to their inclination."

"I'm not surprised. That would be out of character for a person who practices…whatever it is you do."

If he wasn't mistaken, she was fishing. "Once the tour starts, I'll watch you and take notes on your stage performance. Live music has less influence than it did in past decades, but everyone loves the personal touch. I assume your meet and greets are set up?"

She leaned back against the headrest. "You changed the subject."

Her voice was so weary his stomach contracted. Jessica Baker was in the prime of her youth, a talented, beautiful woman whom life had not yet affected. She shouldn't be acting like the world settled around her shoulders as a young girl and never let go.

"I'm not what's important. We're discussing your career, not my private life."

She shifted in her seat. In profile she was even more appealing, with her blonde hair falling across her cheek and making her even younger than she was. He didn't need the reminder of her age. Ten years might be nothing to some, but it mattered to him.

"Right. I'm just your new job."

He was glad he'd chosen to wear glasses that night. They made it easier for him to hide. Things had to be this way. He had a life to rebuild and had no time for gorgeous, intriguing artists. No matter how much her delicate scent enticed him. "That's what Shatter Sound is paying me for."

Her fingers drummed on the windowsill in a beat that reminded him of his past signees when they were hearing a song in their mind. She was a fascinating woman, this too-young enigma.

"Got it. Loud and clear."

They were almost to her apartment, and he had nothing to say. Rather, nothing he should.

When he parked in the red zone nearest to her building, Kai put on the emergency brake, breathing in the scent of Jess all around him. He caught the faint whiff of the alcohol mixing with her breath. Despite the invitation stamped on his companion, he couldn't touch her.

"No good-night wishes, Kai? Not even a hug?"

The desire that surged through him at the idea of tasting her lips made his words harsher than he intended.

"You've had too much to drink. It wouldn't be right."

"I…whatever." She pushed onto the sidewalk and slammed the car door with a heavy thud.

He watched as she went up the street to the main entrance, then punched in a security code and pushed open the door. Her hands were steady when she went through the door.

He waited until she was inside before leaving. She didn't need him to watch her. Kai could leave—he had done his duty.

He drove away, his stomach roiling.

****

She'd been drunk. That was her excuse. Not so much as to be out of control, but enough to cross several boundaries. She didn't often drink, for this reason among many. Nothing good came of overindulging in alcohol. Jess, more than many, was aware of that unassailable fact.

The night had been intoxicating in the dark cabin of his SUV. Kai said nothing, just gazed at her as the silence continued. She wished she could forget what happened next. The words echoed all around her, taunting her with her foolishness.

"No good-night wishes, Kai? Not even a hug?"

Kai had caught his breath and, if she wasn't mistaken, was going to take her up on her offer. His glorious full lips had parted, and he'd leaned closer before pulling back and staring straight ahead. "You've had too much to drink. It wouldn't be right."

Jess moaned and rolled over, covering her head with the pillow.

From the slant of the sun, she estimated the time to be about nine o'clock. The house was quiet with no audible evidence of Michelle in the living room. Then Jess remembered that Michelle was going to a Dodger game with friends.

The bell rang, identifying the thing that had woken her. She sat up and was relieved when the room continued to stay stationary.

Whoever the intruders were, they would go away if she pretended not to be home. She noted her message light was blinking and glanced over. Kai's name showed over a text.

—I want to talk. Let me in. Please.—

Jess pushed off the bed. She was going to answer the door and couldn't kid herself that she was not. She donned a Ryder T-shirt and leggings before going to the intercom. "Contrary to popular belief, Kai, nobody dies from humiliation. They wish they had, but the disease isn't fatal. Go away. I'm fine."

"Let me in."

She took her finger off the button and leaned her head on the wall.

The bell rang again, longer this time, its harsh buzz sharp.

Jess jammed the device on again. "Leave me alone. Wasn't last night enough?"

"I want to talk. I am here in peace. I promise."

"If I don't?" His chuckle sent prickles of awareness through her body.

"The entry code has been punched in so many times the silver is worn off the buttons. It would be child's play to figure it out. Let me in. Either way, I'll be up there soon."

"Give me a minute."

She rushed into the bathroom and brushed her teeth.

A finger comb through her straight hair got the worst of the tangles out and made the bedhead subside.

She went back to the intercom and paused. Then, with a sigh, Jess pressed the entry button. Not too long after, the elevator whirred. Her heart thudded in her chest when his knock sounded at her door. She yanked open the door and stood there, arms crossed.

He had glasses on again, the wireless frames gleaming in the light, but his black hair was down. This morning he'd added color to his wardrobe, a Hawaiian shirt in blues and greens that appeared authentic. She blinked at the assault of pattern.

A brown bag from Noah's Bagels was in his hand, and she fixed on it. "What's that?"

"A peace offering. Can I come in?"

Jess watched him enter her living room for the second time in twenty-four hours. He moved like a cat, fluid grace and rippling muscles uniting in perfect coordination.

"That thing you're wearing is loud."

He put down the bag and riffled through the contents, setting the cream cheese on the counter. "That was the intention. I hoped it would be disarming. It's the real thing." He gestured to the paper. "I bring offerings. I hope you like bagels, or are you on a low-carb diet? I can call for something else."

He appeared tentative and uneasy, his movements fidgety as he focused on the wall behind her.

"I watch my weight but never met a bagel I could say no to." She retrieved plates, a sharp cutting knife, and two butter knives from the kitchen before joining him.

"I am careful about my food," she continued. "I have to be. But as you make a habit of pointing out, I'm young enough that it's not difficult to keep it off."

"Jess..."

She busied herself with selecting a sesame seed bagel and slathering whipped cream cheese on it. "I'm a quick learner, Kai. I got it. You're not attracted to me. That's all that has to be said."

"It's not a question of attraction. One of us needs to be smart. I'm older, so it's me. I'm flattered, Jess. You're a beautiful woman. But it's not a good idea."

****

Liar. His dreams had been haunted by images of her sleek legs wrapped around his waist as he buried his aching body inside her. By the touch of her lips as they parted for his tongue. One brush of her soft skin on his last night and he'd been hard for her.

Her wounded expression had kept him from sleeping. She hadn't been like a woman used to luring men into her bed with a crook of her finger. She was perfect, the all-American female.

It didn't make sense. A piece had to be missing— something he wasn't privy to. Nothing in her background online matched this haunted woman.

He focused on Jess, belatedly aware she was speaking.

"Got it." She gave him a tremulous smile that wavered on the verge of sadness. "Can we be friends? I think you're interesting."

Her response hit him low in the solar plexus. Another woman would have been furious and refused to have anything to do with him. Or tossed him out on his ear and yelled at him for being an idiot.

Jess asked to be his friend.

"I'd like that." He would *not* say more. He could not.

She stared down. Her hair swept forward, covering her face. "Thanks."

He blinked. "For what?"

"Someone else would have slept with me and waited until the morning to tell me we had no future." By the continued downward slant of her head, the effort cost her.

Her words shot through him like a blow.

"It wouldn't have been the first time. Now I expect nothing and get that back in return. I'm not after true love, Kai, but I bet that's your MO. You are not the casual type."

The idea that anyone took this woman for granted filled him with quiet hatred.

He motioned her over to the couch and sat next to her. With his index finger he lifted her chin. The widening of her pupils betrayed her attraction, although she kept her face neutral.

"You're right. I don't indulge in sex on a whim." When he said it like that, he sounded like a jerk.

"Yeah, I got that."

Damn it. She should have been glib and offhand, not wounded. Her careful expression suggested how much his rebuff had hurt her.

Kai leaned down and almost kissed her. He wanted to—so much. The way her eyes widened and breath caught suggested that she wouldn't refuse him. He shouldn't. He couldn't. If he did so, without being able to give her more, he was a tease, or worse.

"You're beautiful, Jess," he said. "Don't let anyone treat you without care. That includes yourself. You are worth more than that."

Those fantastic eyes were huge in her face. He

cursed under his breath again.

"Any man would be honored that you were interested in him." He forced himself to move to the far side of the couch. "Myself included. However, you and I need to work together, and a physical relationship will muddy the waters. Neither of us can afford that. I'll take you up on that offer of friendship. I will warn you I take those ties to heart as well."

Never mind that he might be responsible for her demise at the label, if he didn't like what he discovered on tour. The burden lay heavy on his shoulders. He'd done that dirty deed, as the owner of Apposite, but this was Jess, and that made it different.

"I guess there's nothing informal about Kai Halara. Despite the shirt."

"No." He selected a bagel. "I think that there isn't much that's laid-back about Jessica Baker either."

What might have been a tiny smile lurked around the edges of her mouth. "Guess we're both right. You have a deal, Mr. Halara."

The idea of what kind of arrangements they could come to left him unable to speak. Or move, for fear of betraying the tightness across his zipper.

He cleared his throat. He needed to say something—anything. "Part of the reason I invited you out was to learn more about you." He hoped his voice sounded normal, but he doubted it. "The more I have a feel for your personality, the more I can help design a professional stage show. And…" He wished he were five years older and in a different profession. Or he was, and he could give a woman like her what she deserved. What she needed, in the most primal way. All of it, deep inside her… "As long as I keep my paws to myself. It's better that way."

"Better for who?"

"Jessica…"

She nodded and leaned in toward him. "I got it. I've just never been around anyone like you."

"Nor I you," he admitted.

She made a short, dismissive, cutting gesture. Kai started in surprise at the quick movement.

"Blondes? We're a dime a dozen."

She is insecure. Most artists were, or pretended to be, but Jess truly didn't understand the impact she had on men.

"Not blondes like you."

"Oh yes, like me. Country is littered with brown-eyed blonde female singers. I'm nothing special."

He grasped her shoulders. She met his gaze with such wounded intensity it took all his training and willpower not to drag her across his lap and kiss her senseless.

The continued tightening of his body told him he'd better get under control and fast. "Never say that. Everyone is unique in their own way. We all have the ability to become greater than we are."

He didn't resist when she placed her hands on his forearms.

"Is that speech part of your philosophy?" Her tone was acerbic with a hint of sarcastic disbelief.

"Yes. But it's also fact. You bring so much light to this world. Embrace your gift. You are a rare and wonderful human being and have a lot to offer if you believe in your talent."

She let out a breath and made a laugh that didn't sound like it held much humor. "I do, but the general public does not. Besides, you don't know me or what makes me tick."

"You have a way with words. Your songs have shades of meaning that takes them out of the ordinary. That doesn't come from nowhere."

"My mediocre numbers suggest whatever I put there isn't resonating."

Jess stayed where she was, and he fought to remind himself why he had to keep away.

"That's their loss, not yours. As for the rest, intimacy is not measured in time. It's the depth of the connection."

When she moved her fingers over his skin, Kai couldn't help his harsh exhalation of breath at her caress.

"But…" Her tone was surprised at his muffled gasp. "You're not attracted to me."

He longed to kiss her with a force that stunned him. "I said it wasn't a good idea. Jessica, you would have to be blind or stupid not to comprehend I find you attractive. I'm asking you as a new friend to move away. Please."

If she didn't do as he asked, he wasn't sure how long he could hold on to his control. Her lips trembled, and he had never wanted to throw caution to the winds so much. He could imagine the taste of her, the press of her flesh to his, and the soft fall of her hair over his body.

If she didn't break off contact, he couldn't say what he would do next.

Jess moved back from him and rose, clearing the crumb-dotted plates and dirty knives, busying herself with anything but him.

"I'll meet you in the office tomorrow, to help with your promos."

She gave him a lost glance that almost took his feet out from under him.

"Sure. Yeah. Tomorrow."

Chapter Four

The next day, when Kai arrived at the office, Gordon acknowledged him with little more than a semi-polite nod. In this industry, a time could come when Kai would rise to power again, and it wouldn't pay to be too unpleasant. For now, Gordon had Kai to do his dirty work, and could run the bus over him if necessary.

Dirk and Gordon were the remaining occupants in the room. Kai wasn't sure why the label boss's presence was required. This was standard, basic promotion. Dirk wasn't even needed, though it made more sense for him to be there.

Jess was doing promos via videoconferencing—acting the part of rising young star. If she didn't yet fit that label, she could pretend.

Once again, she was wearing a dress. This one was a pastel yellow with a high collar, but had a plunging neckline and a hem that fell to two inches above her knees. It nipped in at the waist and accentuated her bodice with cloth-covered buttons the same color as the dress. The sight of her bare legs inflamed Kai, and he was grateful a table stood between him and where she was taking the calls.

Dirk Roberts moved next to Kai as Jess ended the call. Faint lines of exhaustion marred her face. If Kai were a different man, he would take her into his arms and carry her out of there.

Her life. Her choice.

"Being charming takes its toll," she said to the crowd, but her focus was on Kai. At the sight of him, she brightened, her face lighting from within.

Damn it.

The time on the road would mean enforced intimacy, a dangerous proximity where many did things they wouldn't under normal circumstances. He would have to watch himself.

Kai waved a hand at her. "If that's true, it doesn't show. You have a charisma that carries you through."

Her breath hitched at his words. Before she could speak, Dirk's rumbling voice rang out.

"You did great, darlin'. You're a natural with those folks."

She gave Dirk a quick glance that might have been pleasure and might have been wariness. Dirk's baggage, as well as his size, made him a target. Kai discounted such things. In Hollywood, rumors, and fame, came and went.

Nonetheless, nobody should call Jess *darlin'* unless his name was Kai.

He had to get under control. If asked, he would have insisted he was a modern man, but now he could be sure of nothing. He hadn't been irrational as a matter of course until Jessica Baker came along.

"We're done here." Gordon closed the gap to Jessica, pushing past Dirk and Kai as he did so. He had a brittle quality, and Kai wondered what was troubling him. When he shot a quick glance at Dirk, Kai decided that Gordon's odd mood was not directed at him.

"Whatever you say, boss. I'll get back to it once Jess is finished, if we've got nothing further here."

Kai had been the boss for so long that he assumed Dirk meant himself for a minute until he saw that Dirk was referring to Gordon. The man grunted and nodded in a gruff gesture. Kai wasn't used to being under someone else's whims.

Gordon separated from Jessica and gestured to Dirk. "I'll meet you in your office. I have some things I'd like you to give me your opinion on."

Dirk inclined his head, a muscle jumping in the back of his jaw. Jess was still where she'd been when the call ended, packing up her stuff. Smudges showed through the heavy makeup, betraying her weariness. Her eyes shone from her face, more honey than chocolate and as delicious as either sweet.

"You are very pretty today, Jess." Kai swallowed down the additional words that fought to be said. "Yellow is a good color on you."

Dirk snorted something that might have been laughter, but Kai had no idea what the joke might be. The soft curves of her breasts were visible in the décolletage that was low but not so low as to be too revealing. Just enough to give a man a glimpse of heaven and make him beg to do anything to get her to spend time with him.

Except she'd done that, and he had tossed it aside.

"Thanks. My roommate doesn't share your opinion, but I'll go with your assessment. I tried to mirror the yellow T-shirts that Dirk designed for the tour. Yellow was an interesting choice, but they've been flying off the site, so the color was a good idea."

Dirk started to raise his hand to his head as though touching the brim of a hat but let it fall away. His shift in expression suggested he was remembering a different topic. "Good luck on the tour. I'll be in touch, but call me if you need anything."

"Thanks, Dirk. We'll be back soon enough."

He held out his hand to Kai, and they shook before Dirk retreated. Gordon followed without speaking to Kai or Jess.

Whatever was going on had little to do with Kai. He was a temp and was here until he could get back on his feet again, and then he was gone. Little snubs, small hurts, they meant nothing. To him.

If someone hurt Jessica, that would evoke a different reaction.

****

She wished he had pulled his hair back and worn his glasses, but today he had it loose and his glasses stowed. Jess had nowhere to hide from his too penetrating gaze and mysterious aura.

Kai bowed and turned his hand, palm up, in her direction. "Good job. You were very poised."

She walked to him as Dirk and Gordon took their leave. They didn't pay Jess any attention, which she didn't mind. Not when Kai was there to focus on.

Lusting after him was not going to do any of them any good.

"I was scared to death," she admitted. "Thanks for not noticing." She fought not to lean over and put her mouth on his. Just taste his lips and glory in their warmth under hers. The temptation was so strong she had started to move in before she drew back.

"You don't show it, which is all that matters. I've watched you perform online. You're very good. As I've said, your songs have more depth than you're admitting to, though that may not be visible to all. You slip in the poignancy, which is what makes a great artist. I am sure

I will recommend some changes to your onstage persona, but I won't have an answer for that until I have been to some of your shows. One thing I don't have to deal with is a bloated ego. If anything, you sell yourself short, which is a rare quality in a performer. I'd like to break through to that inner core and give the real Jessica to the world."

He slipped the matter-of-fact compliments in with so little change in his tone that she couldn't decide whether to thank him or let it alone. His idea to expose her vulnerable side was not going to happen. Those emotions were private and for songs, not interviews. The truth about her was limited to her trusted circle and not for public display.

"I'd rather not talk about any of that. That's not what I'm getting paid for. They are after the fantasy. This." She gestured to her body encased in the yellow dress. "They moon over the golden girl but not Jessica Baker. It's a good thing I wasn't on your label after all. I doubt any of your leftover Apposite tchotchkes would suit me. Judging from that monstrosity you call a watch, I bet all your T-shirts are dark and scary—like you. I'm the opposite. I keep it light. It's better that way."

Kai threw back his head and laughed. Heat surged through her on a wave that made her dizzy. Her vision blurred as the desire to stroke him washed over her.

"Nice deflection. I guess I deserved that after last night. You're correct. I have about fifty Apposite T-shirts in storage, and they are all black with the logo lightning bolt. Much too dark and baggy for your gorgeous body."

His compliments always came out sounding reluctant. As he took a step back, she wondered if he regretted coming with her. He had no obligation to do so. He wasn't under contract.

"There's something we should discuss."

His solemn tone made Jess swallow and meet his gaze. She'd had men she was attracted to not be interested in her, though often they offered one night of sex as their compromise. She had sometimes taken them up on that. That was fine with her. Sex was fun, and love was not always the endgame. She doubted the serious Kai Halara would agree.

She wouldn't either, if he were the man in question.

"It's about Ryder Bingham."

The look on his face was so intense that as much as she longed to bathe in the heat, a part of her also ached to run. Her attraction to him was too extreme, too overpowering. She didn't have time for this. "Ryder? What about him?"

He cleared his throat, his dark hair falling forward. If she wasn't mistaken, his hands shook in minute tremors.

She didn't dare hope he felt anywhere near the emotions she had.

"Are you two an item? Is that why he chose you for the tour?"

She would have smiled if not for the heat running through her veins. "That has nothing to do with it. Yes, we had a thing, but just one night. The time we were together, Ryder told me beforehand he couldn't give me anything more and we shouldn't go forward if I needed true love. I said that was good because I didn't have time for more." She was sure Kai wouldn't believe her next statement, but said it anyway. "Don't get me wrong, I was attracted to Ryder then and still like him, but we were just for that night. Getting into a relationship was never in the cards." She paused, searching for the right words to bolster her impressions of the singer. "He has a piece missing, like a tragedy happened to him long ago that left him scarred for life. That's the closest I can come to explaining it."

"I'm sorry about his past but pleased that you are not more than that." Kai held out his hand to Jess.

She feared her reaction if she so much as moved. She shook her head and gestured to the hallway where the muffled noises of office life were discernable. So many questions beat through her mind. Ones without answers, or at least none she could bear to face.

"Ryder is Ryder. We're not going to have an issue because he and I slept together, are we? We had fun, but neither of us were ever trying to make it into more. I am not the kind of woman who appreciates being guilted over sex, Kai, so if you're that type, we can end this conversation right now."

His pupils widened, and his throat moved as he swallowed. She already regretted her flare of temper. She'd learned young to keep her head down and deflect when adults got belligerent. In her line of work, she had to play coy more often than engage in a full-frontal assault.

Full frontal with Kai. The two of them, skin to skin... The talk of sex had reminded her of his strong body when she'd tried to throw herself at him—and gotten tossed on her ass for her trouble.

"I didn't mean..." He stuttered to a halt before raking his hand through his hair. The straight tresses fell back into place after he did so.

She was certain he didn't use much in the way of

products. Some, perhaps. He was well-groomed, in his way.

As fast as it came, her flare of temper left. It wasn't his fault he didn't desire her. If the situations had been reversed, she would be well within her rights to tell him to back off. She had to do the same to her own flaring libido.

"Forget it. No harm done. I should head home. I've got to make sure I've got everything I need for the start of the tour."

He inclined his head. "I'll walk you out."

They went to the parking lot in silence, each with their hands clasped behind their backs. Jess didn't trust herself not to touch him if they weren't clasped, but couldn't begin to speculate about why Kai kept his tucked away.

At her car door he gazed at her with, if she was not mistaken, a tinge of regret. Perhaps that was her imagination. It wouldn't be the first thing she'd imagined about him.

"Good night, Jess. Until the start of the tour, aloha." He moved as though to hug her and then stepped back. He gave her a bow before pivoting on his heel and striding away.

Chapter Five

The bus was idling in the Shatter Sound parking lot. Jess kept peering out the window and checking her phone, frowning as the minutes ticked by. Her guitarist and keyboard player were, as usual, late. She grew frustrated when people weren't prompt.

Kai had been on time. Of course he had. She struggled not to run to him when he emerged from his rideshare, rolling luggage behind him.

He climbed the bus stairs and motioned to the bunks, asking without words which was his. She had been tempted to give him one next to hers but decided to be smart and pointed out one away from her. Within minutes the rest of the band arrived, filling the bus with noise and commotion. Jess was swept into a text discussion about last-minute details with Rick, her tour manager. Kai sat cross-legged on his bunk, watching the interaction with no expression on his face. His gaze moved between the various players, weighing, evaluating.

Judging. Them—and her.

Kai's shuttered glance landed on Jess as the men got louder and louder. She flicked her eyes back to the guys and fought not to say anything. She had found in these situations things went better if she was "one of them" and ignored any adolescent behavior. They were a good group, and the antics had tapered off as the band got comfortable with her. The presence of a newcomer had to have inspired their acting out.

"Got drinks here—Jessie?" Trevor, the fiddle player, moved to toss her one, but she shook her head.

"Too early."

"What about you, new guy?"

Kai made a negative motion.

"Sorry we're late." Benny said the statement while he was grabbing for one of the beers, though he didn't look contrite.

"You wouldn't be you if you got places on time." Jessica struggled to control her pique, aware that her being out of sorts had less to do with their lateness and more to do with the one who had gotten there ahead of schedule.

The arrival of the guitar player meant they could be off. Once the bus door hissed shut, their driver put the vehicle into gear, and it lurched forward. The trip to San Diego would take a little over two hours. The plan was to get there at noon and load in before Jess' soundcheck. Ryder was already set up, and Jess would arrange her instruments in front of his more complicated arrangement. She'd done this sort of tour over a dozen times since she'd gotten signed to Shatter Sound, but this time was different. All because of Kai Halara.

She was insane.

"Time for Jessie to kick our butts in Trivial Pursuit," Tom said. "You in, new guy?"

She would get sick of that nickname in no time, but she said nothing. As with so many past situations, she held her tongue and tried to let their comments roll off her. They might be her band, but she was outnumbered.

Kai stood and stretched. The flex of his powerful

thighs as he straightened his body made her mouth go dry. She coughed and fiddled with her hair, biting the underside of her lip. Kai gave her a quick glance, and she stopped the nervous movement at once. *Never show weakness.* She met his gaze, trying to think of anything besides how well he filled out his jeans.

"After you," he said, gesturing to the game.

She pushed past him, and his heat seared her. All she had to do was shift, and she would touch him. All of him. She would not. She could not.

They sat at the table at the back of the bus. The Trivial Pursuit game was already set up, and Tom handed her the blue disk.

"Her favorite color," Tom said.

"I got it."

Benny snickered when Kai was forced to choose between the pink and yellow disks, but a quick noise from Jess stopped him.

Kai selected the yellow disk and placed it in front of him. "It's yellow, like your dress."

Her breath caught at Kai's words, but like before, she said nothing.

His clean nails were square and blunt cut. Tiny cuts on his hands were evidence of some sort of outdoor work or manual labor. An olive-green T-shirt accentuated the taut muscles of his body. Compared to the boys in the band, he was the perfect adult male.

The dice clicked on the game board, and Jess focused on Tom. Kai's heat reached her from the short distance separating their chairs. The remaining members were on one of the free bunks, playing poker.

Life on the road. The simple fact of life as a musician. Album sales were great, and videos got an artist exposure, but the slog of getting out and performing for fans helped keep Jess in the forefront of their minds. In this day of a plethora of consumable art, singers struggled to stand out. She had learned in her early days as a fan that she always remembered the ones who were dismissive or cruel to her. She would never forget being twelve years old and running into a music icon at a grocery store. When a shy, trembling Jess asked for the larger-than-life icon's autograph, the woman had whirled on Jess, anger flashing, and then demanded her bodyguard get Jess away from her. Later, she understood the pressure that had caused the woman's behavior that day, but she hadn't been aware at the time. She'd held that bitter memory inside her for years until she realized the truth.

"Your turn," Kai said, handing the dice to her. His fingers brushed over her palm, and Jess suppressed a shiver.

Kai's was the one disk that had moved more than a handful of spaces. While she zoned out, they had been playing the game—and Kai was ahead.

When Kai grunted after Jess got the history question right, a grin played over the corners of her mouth.

Yellow, like your dress.

"She's a shark," Benny said. "She kicks all our asses in Trivial Pursuit."

Jess wrinkled her nose at him, and Benny stuck his tongue out at the singer.

"Is that so?" Kai met her gaze with a sexier-than-hell glint in his eyes. "You're full of surprises, Jessica Baker."

The gesture turned her bones to jelly. "Yes." She shook out her hair, trying to quell the desire rising inside her. "I am."

****

The dark expanse of the Pacific Ocean gleamed. Seagulls wheeled in circles, their cacophonous cries echoing around the sand and scrub. A handful of beachgoers dotted the surf in the late afternoon, accompanied by distant shouts. Kai took a step closer, the ancient call of the water tugging at him. He'd grown up on an island, and the ocean was a part of him. The tang of salt cut the air, and a stiff breeze blew off the vast briny expanse nearby.

"Nice place." He nodded at the sand and surf that lay beyond the venue. "I've never booked a band here. I was missing out."

"Yeah, it doesn't suck," Benny interjected. "The girls are cute too."

Jess swatted Benny on the arm. "You think lampposts are cute."

"They are!" Benny grinned at her even while he undid the doors to the storage bins at the bottom of the bus. The crew began taking gear out of the compartments with practiced movements.

Ryder's two buses were parked a short distance away, their engines idling. Kai could make out nothing through the darkened windows and shaded his eyes to get a better look. As he did so, the hydraulic door to the first one opened and a brown-haired figure showed in the entranceway. He zeroed in on Jess and waved to her.

"Jess!"

"Ryder!"

Kai's breath tightened. This man had been intimate with her in a way Kai dreamed of. He watched as Ryder hauled her into his arms. Kai's spine relaxed when he noted Ryder held her and released her almost at once—too fast for lingering emotions.

The singer's gaze fell on Kai, and he separated from Jess. "I'm Ryder Bingham." He held out his hand.

"Kai Halara."

"The guy who ran Apposite. Sure. Sorry about your label."

"Thanks."

Kai was surprised the popular singer had even been aware of Apposite, and was more amazed he was conscious it had gone under. Jess and Ryder stood a companionable distance apart, comfortable but not close. He could discern no indication that their brief involvement had wounded either one of them.

Still, the idea that this man had a prior situationship with Jess made Kai glower.

"Too bad you didn't sign country. It might have been fun to be part of your ensemble."

Kai uttered a sound somewhere between a snort and a cough. "Apposite was a tiny company, and you would have outgrown it in no time. You're with Earthy Cry. A label that size can do far more for you than I could have."

Ryder stepped back from both of them, his hands tucked into his back pockets. He was a handsome man, with an expensive haircut, a rugged face, and eyes a shade darker than Jess'.

They would have incredible children. Their kids would be attractive and talented. Jess should find a man like Ryder and hold on to him. She shouldn't be interested in a failed executive that was too old for her.

Then again, Ryder wasn't much younger than him.

"I am with Earthy Cry Records right now, but..." Ryder's voice was careful and noncommittal. "If I have been informed of the rumors, so were you. There's a shakeup imminent. The new president isn't a country guy."

"I hope it works out. Many labels will be there to pick up the pieces if Earthy Cry releases you."

Pain crossed Ryder's face and then was replaced by a grin. "That's kind of you to say. I think Shatter Sound has a contract lined up if it falls apart. Although…maybe not. Too soon to tell."

Kai allowed himself a pang of regret that he couldn't offer Ryder a deal if his current recording contract fell apart, and then let it slide. Karma was karma, and he couldn't do much to change it.

"Jess, do you need help loading in?" He waved to where the band and crew were dealing with the gear.

She glanced at the emptying bus. "We're good. They have this down to a science. Why?"

He gestured at the open expanse of sand, the sea calling to him. "I'm going to work out at the beach."

****

The vision would have been amazing captured for posterity.

After setting up their equipment, Jess told herself she should practice, rehearse, run, do something that didn't involve the beach. When her body refused to obey her mind, she headed for the sand. She'd never had a choice. Like a moth to a flame, she was going to where Kai was.

When she found him in a secluded area, he was clad in white pants and a tunic in the same color, belted with a black sash around his waist. His feet were bare, and his hair was loose as he moved to an unseen rhythm.

The combination of his dark hair, stark white

Claire Davon

clothing, and gleaming golden sun setting over the ocean created an image that would forever be seared into her mind.

As she lurked, he pivoted and cried out. Then he kicked his leg up and out in a forward motion, his knee bent and one arm outstretched.

She watched for several minutes while he progressed across the sand. It wasn't until he came to a stop that she got up and closed the distance to him. Kai focused on her, his breathing heavy and his hair tousled. The air around them was thick with moisture—and anticipation.

"Karate?" Jessica gestured to his clothes. She pushed her hair back, the strands catching in her mouth. Then she gave up and let her hair do what it would, just as the breeze was blowing his clothes so they molded to his body. Hard muscles stood out on his chest and thighs, making her long to smooth her hands over him.

"*Shotokan.* It's a style of karate developed in the last century but isn't strictly speaking that particular discipline."

"I don't get the difference, so I'll take your word for it." She moved closer until the rock wall made it like the two of them were alone on the beach. His nearness slid across her senses, rippling through her insides.

"I can teach you, if you like. We offer classes in self-defense."

She met his gaze but, as usual, couldn't determine what he was thinking. Or perhaps she was too afraid to believe. "I work out."

"Running and lifting weights will do nothing when put to the test by a firearm."

"Will your *Shotokan* stop a gun?"

He inclined his head. "Point taken. If you decide to learn, I will show you."

They walked in silence along the space between the wet sand from the oncoming tide and the dry mixture beyond it.

When they reached the hotel parking lot, he stopped.

The contrast of his dark hair on the white fabric of his uniform made her senses soar. She couldn't remember a time when a man had affected her the way he did. "I'm not helpless, Kai, nor am I fragile. I've taken care of myself for a long time. Longer than you would expect."

His gaze was troubled, quick flickers of emotion dancing in their obsidian depths. "You always surprise me. I'm often good at cataloging folks, but you shake my perceptions."

"I do that a lot. Everyone prefers to believe I'm the pretty blonde who grew up with a pom-pom and a designer handbag. Not that there's anything wrong with either. Those women have different stories and traumas, more than likely. That wasn't my story, though." She waited as he went quiet again, his jaw moving.

He took in a deep breath and raked his hand over his hair before the wind took it again. "No. From what I gather, that's far from your situation. It makes things difficult."

Jess' heart fell, and she was sure some of her dismay showed. "I make things difficult for you? That's not a surprise either."

He had the outward signs of every man who had told her she was too complex for them to get involved with, or too serious. "I have so many thoughts lurking in my mind, but I won't say them. Jessica…about Ryder…"

"I thought we covered that, but here we are again. Why? Are you jealous?" The wind tugged at their clothing, but she also stayed where she was.

"No. Yes."

"It's not like that with him. Ryder is broken somehow. He's got a good front, but he's lost. I don't love him. I never will. Like him, respect him, admire him, all those things. Kai, why are you asking again?"

He raked his hands through his hair again. "I pride myself on being honest at all times. I wish I could tell you, but I am not sure."

Though he hadn't given her a real answer, she decided to be content with his words. He said nothing else as they headed back for the hotel and the night ahead.

She wished she had the courage to ask more questions, but Jess had learned a long time ago not to try to uncover anything she wasn't prepared to accept the answer to. From the way Kai walked next to her, there but also far away, whatever he would say in reply wouldn't be good for her ego.

She had no desire to put herself through that.

Chapter Six

During the next two weeks and a half dozen shows, Kai tried to keep his distance from Jess. He watched her perform and took notes, considering all the ways that she might do better. She had a good way with the audience, but he had several recommendations that could bolster her stage presence.

They hadn't discussed it. Perhaps Jess was also staying away from him, as he'd more or less told her to do. He should be grateful, but the perverse side of him was not. Gordon hadn't checked in, but Kai was aware of his obligation to the label. He needed to give Gordon his professional opinion, if the decision hadn't been made.

They were in Laughlin now that the Southern California and Las Vegas shows were done. Ally Wilson had come for the initial outings but had already returned to Los Angeles. She hadn't socialized much with the rest of them, and Kai hadn't pushed it. Whatever was going on with her was her own business.

Kai was watching Jess and the band play the slots, but not participating in the activity. Ryder wasn't around, but two of his band were also in the casino, one playing blackjack and one talking to a fan at the bar.

Kai kept his attention on Jess, who was focused on the machine. If he wasn't mistaken, she darted glances his way when she supposed his attention was engaged elsewhere.

When his phone rang, he recognized the Shatter Sound main number. Ally, perhaps, or Gordon. He might have summoned the label president with his ruminations. He glanced at his watch, startled to discover that they were still within working hours. Time had a way of getting away from a person on the road—and in the casinos.

"Kai Halara." He moved away from the noise and lights of the Laughlin casino and out the sliding doors as he connected to the call. Jess followed his movements, and his heart thudded.

"It's Dirk Roberts. Case the caller ID doesn't tell you."

All he could think about was Jess. Every time he was with her, he became a little more entranced, a little less sure he was doing the right thing by not engaging. She was so beautiful and so interesting. She made him long for things he had no business going after.

"Hello, Dirk." The VP of marketing had no reason to be calling him. Kai held the phone like he might a snake, waiting for the second shoe to drop. Perhaps Gordon had sent Dirk to do his dirty work. He could even release Kai here, in the middle of Nevada, and provide no way for Kai to get home.

Eager gamblers ebbed around him, pushing past him to enter the Laughlin casino. He had never understood the appeal of gambling. The odds were on the side of the house, and the house never lost. When he relayed that sentiment to the singer, Jess had pointed out she could play the penny slots for hours on ten dollars. That made it cheap amusement. Even Kai couldn't argue with that.

"How's the tour going? Jessica doing all right?"

Kai reflected back to watching her perform over the series of shows and the difficult task that lay in front of him. He wondered if Dirk had been told what Gordon was up to. After reflecting over his impressions of the man, Kai didn't believe so. Dirk was much too straight a shooter to deal well with a tactic like Gordon's. "Jess has amazing stage presence—videos don't do her justice. I have some ideas about how to get more out of her, but we should do the entire tour first." He gripped the phone in a tight fist before speaking. "What can I do for you?"

Jess kept peering out the doors whenever they opened. On impulse, Kai moved to stand in front of the entrance. She grinned at the sight of him.

A man could get used to the idea that he was the one thing that mattered.

"The president of Plausive Records is retiring." Dirk's bass tones rang through the line, jerking Kai's attention back to his call.

His hand tightened on the device. "That's definite? All I got so far was rumors. Too bad. It isn't a surprise. From what I understand, he's had some health challenges these last years."

"Yeah. I got the same from my friend there. Thought you'd find it interesting."

Words failed Kai as the memory of the collapse of Apposite surged through him. "Interesting and futile. Plenty will up for the job at Plausive. John has some good employees under him. They wouldn't be interested in me. My label collapsed, and I stopped mattering."

"Labels come and go all the time."

Not mine. My dream fails once.

"They're keeping their options open. My buddy asked about you. I told him y'all was a good man." Dirk paused before continuing. "I'll text you his number for more info. Informational only, or not. Your choice. Unless you like consulting."

"No. Suffice it to say I don't."

Dirk chuckled, the amusement clear through the crackle of the cell phone connection. "Bud, you sure got a formal way of talking."

"English was my father's second language. I learned it from him."

"That explains it. The opportunity is there if you're interested. My guy can set you up. The rest is up to you. I'm available for a reference if you need one."

"Thank you, Dirk. That's very decent of you."

"That's how it's done in my world. Tell me if I can do anything."

Kai signed off after a handful of pleasantries. Then he went back to the casino—and Jess. The noise and flashing lights engulfed him, but all he cared about was the blonde singer feeding coins into a machine, one at a time.

She paused in her slot playing, giving him a quick nod when he arrived. "Business or pleasure?" She watched the wheels spin but gave him a sideways glance that made his breath catch.

"Dirk. He was checking in." Kai didn't examine why he was reluctant to share Dirk's news with her. Perhaps for the same reason he wasn't telling her he might be her judge, jury, and executioner.

The machine spun, and the display whirled as she won, dinging with amassed credits. Jess grinned as it climbed.

When it stopped, Kai nodded once. "You hit the jackpot." He gestured to the display where 4,013 credits were showing.

"I did! Forty bucks! Woo-hoo. Go me." Her golden-blonde hair and tanned skin shone in the flashing lights of the casino, changing colors with the winking movement.

He glanced at his watch. "Why don't you cash out? It's time for sound check. After that, I'll buy you dinner at one of the restaurants here instead of going to the comped buffet again. I bet you're sick of eating hotel food."

"I'll take care of dinner with my winnings." She gazed at him with eyes so luminous he fought not to bend down and kiss her.

He threw his head back and grunted. Hearing her tinkling laugh, he let his head fall forward again, gazing at her from under a curtain of black hair. "Me man, you woman. Me get you food."

She folded her arms and glared at him, but amusement sparkled in her eyes. Jess was so delightful that he… Kai pushed away that thought.

"You're a liberated, modern Buddhist, Kai Halara. Shut up and let me treat."

"Well." He gestured in the direction of the restaurants. "Since you put it that way, lead the way, Jessica Baker."

****

Kai was…distracting. That was the way to describe his impact on her. He observed her from the front, checking their interactions. Jess was having trouble focusing on anything else. First, he watched her cross the stage and back again. Then he vanished, to return by the sound booth. Then he was gone from there. Heat flooded her body. She was glad she had good reflexive memory, or she would have forgotten what she was singing, where she was, and why she was where she was. Instead, she was still performing to songs that she couldn't remember writing. She ran, she pointed, and she toyed with the crowd by rote, all her attention focused on the man that kept shifting positions, never staying in one spot for too long.

The feminine part of her wished his scrutiny was more personal than professional, but this was his job. That was what he had been brought in to do. She'd been told he excelled at anything he tried to do—except his label.

He might be excelling on getting her released. She had to remember that.

After she wound down her set, Jess watched some of Ryder's before finding her way to her merchandise table. Though few were in the lobby, she sat at the table with a pen in hand, prepared for anyone who might buy one of her items. She was alone with her merch guy, making small talk, until Ryder's set ended.

Patrons swarmed out, chattering and breathless, descending on the merch tables with intent. The line for Ryder's was long, with fewer approaching Jess. Kai had come out and was standing to the side. When the crush began, he moved to the back, out of the way.

Way more eager followers were at Ryder's table, but a respectable amount of people had gathered to purchase Jess' items. She had donned a red sleeveless tank top that said "Jessica Baker" in slanted script style across the front. Though she longed to focus on Kai, this was her job. The man was taking up far too much space in her mind. She had to pay attention to the task at hand.

A memory flooded her even as she signed

autographs and posed with fans. She had been fifteen and was going to an open mike audition with her guitar and a dream. Her parents, plowed as was typical for a Friday night, asked her to give them money for booze. She explained that the money she had was for the entrance fee, but they attempted to wheedle it out of her. They even tried to take her guitar so they could pawn it. Her brother, Rocky, who had arrived to take her to the event, intervened before things got out of hand. He handed them cash and then gave them a disgusted sniff as he took Jess' arm to lead her to his car.

She'd done well that night, but her parents had never asked—nor cared. They hadn't remembered the events in the morning, or said they didn't. Jess was never sure of the truth.

She had been signing autographs and posing for pictures without being conscious of what she was doing. That wasn't fair. These were new fans and with luck could become loyal ones. No musings about her early life. She had to focus on the here and now.

She beamed at the next fan, a young, attractive man in his mid-twenties, with such force he gave her a lopsided grin in return.

Then the man leaned over the table and bent his mouth to her ear. "Make it out to Russ. And…" He slipped his hand into his jacket and placed a piece of paper in her hand. "Here's my digits if you're at loose ends tonight."

Jess turned her best noncommittal yet welcoming expression at Russ and signed the CD liner notes. "Thank you."

****

Damn it. She was flirting with the fans. The man

slipped a note into Jess' palm, and Kai had a sudden urge to step forward, yank him from the crowd, and tear him to pieces.

What she was doing was good PR. Any artist worth his or her salt would do the same. Those people weren't Jess.

He watched the line move, trying to dissect her interaction with those buying her CDs and T-shirts for her to sign. She had a natural sensuality, an earthy female quality that made him ache. Jessica was compelling, with an open, honest appreciation for everyone she encountered that made men long to get close to her.

It made *him* need to get close to her.

The fact that she hadn't glanced his way for over a half hour was driving Kai crazy. He had no right to behave this way, yet the primitive side of him wished to stake his claim.

He watched the line move. The majority of the women weren't interested in anything more than Jess' autograph, but most of the men lingered. They would lean in closer, ask something that required her to respond. Then there were the pictures. The men would step behind the table and put their arms around her, too close and too intimate, and then push into her with their big "she digs me" grins as they mugged for the camera.

Die. They all needed to die.

Kai almost turned away from the tableau, shocked at the savagery of his emotions, before forcing himself to stay where he was. Jess picked him out of the darkness and smiled at him, then she gave her attention to yet one more new male fan begging for her attention.

No. He moved forward. *Me. Pay attention to me.*

Though a muscle jumped in his jaw, Kai forced

himself to calm down and think like the rational human he was. Jess was doing what was necessary, and as much as it upset him, she was right. He'd given her so many mixed signals that she might have put her attraction to the side to focus on what was important.

He needed to stay focused. Plausive Records could be a way out of the sinkhole he had gotten himself into, and to become relevant again. Perhaps even help struggling artists' careers, like Jess'. If Shatter Sound dropped her, maybe Plausive could step in. The problem was that they, like his old label Apposite, did not deal in country music.

There could always be a first time. If he got the job, of course.

In the meantime, the woman in question was flirting with her fans, showing no sign that Kai was there at all. Perhaps he'd pushed it too far, and Jessica Baker, who had no dearth of available men, had lost interest in the one who said he couldn't give her anything more.

The idea that Jess had stopped desiring him was intolerable.

****

Tony was packing up her unsold items when Kai approached her.

She'd tried ignoring him, and all Kai had done was retreat further. He didn't care. He was just one more unattainable guy. Like Craig, who'd fled when the situation got tough. Like any number of lovers before him.

Like her parents.

"I'd like to buy a T-shirt." Kai handed exact change to Tony. He reached for an extra-large dark-gray T-shirt that said "Jess" on the front.

"You don't need to." She needed sleep and the reset that dreams brought. Perhaps tomorrow she would have an idea how to deal with the enigma that was Kai Halara. Right now, it all was too big.

"I do. I want you to sign it too."

"I'll give you one." Anything to make him leave. She could go to her bus—their bus—and go to bed, pretending he wasn't there. Fat chance.

"No. That's bad marketing. If a customer is willing to pay, you take their money."

Tony handed Kai the shirt. She met Kai's gaze while Tony packed the rest of the merch up and wheeled it off on his dolly.

She should go—now. This ridiculous infatuation had to stop. Hadn't she learned from her past? The one person she could depend on was herself. Everyone else let her down.

"Jess."

Kai was standing in front of the table, his new T-shirt and her pen held out to her. The pen quivered in his shaking fingers.

"Jess, please."

She took the items from him but had no idea what to say. "I can't imagine what you're asking of me." Though she tried to suppress it, her hurt showed in the clipped sounds.

He drew back at her irritated words. Before he could take the pen from her, she snatched it out of his reach.

Casino workers began taking the tables away. Jess and Kai stayed silent until all that was left of their presence was a pathway to the river and litter behind them.

She handed the unsigned T-shirt and the pen back to

him. He tucked the pen into his pocket and looped the T-shirt around his wrist.

"Let's walk. I've never been to this area before." Kai gestured to the water twinkling ahead of them.

The path along the Riverwalk followed the water. They watched the barges float down with their LED lights on the side. He stopped by the iron fence leading to the river. Jess tilted her head up and studied him. His face flickered in and out in time to their display, dappling him in light and darkness.

Kai Halara was a mystery, and she didn't like those. She could never be certain until a guy said what he was thinking. Even then, they lied. She'd learned that a long time ago.

We promise we'll pay you back on Friday.

That Friday, like so many through her years, had ended in two wasted parents and a hungry Jessica whose lunch money for the week had been stolen. Borrowed.

I won't hurt you, Jess. I'm here for you.

That, right before Craig broke up with her. She didn't blame him, not really, but he'd still walked away and left her alone.

A barge honked its horn, making Jess jump. She brushed against Kai. His jaw tightened, and she wondered if he felt the desire running through her at the simple contact as much as she did.

She doubted it.

"Jessica…"

He stilled with a hand on her arm, and she faced him.

"Yes, Kai?" She didn't dare hope.

"This is madness." He took her in his arms. He held her in the darkness cut by the occasional spotlight of the barge. "Tonight was painful. Watching you flirt after the show brought emotions out in me that… Jess."

Just the one word was enough to stir her desire to life. "I'm not sure I believe that. What kind of emotions?"

"Too many to name. I have to kiss you. Please."

"Yes."

He gathered her close, tasting the curve of her lips before pushing into her mouth. Kai tasted like passion and promise. His strong hands gripped her waist as he leaned into her, the spicy scent of his cologne tantalizing her senses. The feel of his lips against hers was every fantasy she'd had in the night and every waking fever dream. Subtle heat radiated from his body, making her long to stroke his skin—all of it. Tingling ran down her hands and into her core when she touched him, the sensation radiating through her.

The kiss was brief—much too so for her liking. Jess wanted to press forward and taste him again. And again. She let out a reluctant sigh and accepted it when Kai pulled back. His dark eyes were unreadable in the night. He uttered something that might have been her name before putting her head on his chest and resting his head on the top of hers.

She never wished to move again. She was going to get her heart broken, but she would worry about that some other time. Happiness was a fleeting thing anyway, and she'd learned long ago to deal with crumbs.

If the crumbs came attached to Kai Halara, she'd take them.

Chapter Seven

They were about to board Jess' bus when her cell phone rang. A quick glance at the display told her Ryder was calling. She stopped, and Kai paused and waited when she tapped on his back.

"Ryder, hi. We were just about to head out."

"I'm glad I caught you before you did. You and Kai care to join me? I could use some company besides old Bart here."

The air smelled of diesel and concrete. Inside, the guys were waiting for Jess.

"Ryder is asking if we are interested in traveling with him." She didn't say anything about Ryder's unspoken assumption that they were together.

"I'd like that." She might have been mistaken, but a pleased smile tugged at Kai's lips. She wished she were causing that amusement—or kissing those lips.

Ryder's bus had a video screen, couches, and a table and chairs just like hers, albeit bigger and more state of the art. The perks of success.

"Be it ever so mobile, there's no place like home." Ryder gestured to a whiskey bottle and shot glasses on the table near the couches.

The driver shut the door and revved the engine, then eased away from the venue, heading to the next destination.

When Kai drew in a ragged breath, Jess frowned.

She needed about an hour to unwind, but he hadn't been performing. The man got up with the sun and did his *Shotokan* workouts before dawn broke. Or went running on the beach. Or any number of activities that started around the time she went to sleep.

"Don't wait up for us. Ryder and I can talk until we get tired."

"I was hoping to share some liquor with you," Ryder murmured. "Even though you're not a big drinker, surely you won't deny one tragic musician the courtesy of tasting Kentucky's finest? I'd sure appreciate it if you did, unless you don't drink for other reasons."

Jess shook her head, giving Kai another uncertain glance.

"I'm fine." Kai patted the space next to him on the couch.

Ryder took the chair across from them. "Sit. That's a very nice whiskey, and it would be a shame to waste it." He poured shots and handed them to the pair. "A toast. To friends and new beginnings." He met Kai's gaze and then winked at Jess.

Heat pricked her cheeks, and she shifted her attention down. Jess and Kai tilted their glasses to Ryder and drank. She moved her calf to push into Kai's, and he didn't shift away.

She shouldn't be doing this. Yet she was.

"That's a fine liquor," Kai said, watching Ryder pour another shot. "Perfect for tonight."

"Have you ever been married, Kai?" Ryder asked.

Kai took a sip of his whiskey. "I have not. You?"

"No." Ryder pointed at Jess with a tilt of the glass. "I have been told straight from the horse's mouth that Jess hasn't. Have you been in love, Kai?"

Ryder must have had some whiskey before they came on board. If not, she couldn't imagine him asking a complete stranger questions like this.

Kai leaned forward and studied him. "Twice. The first time when I was twenty-two, the sort of first love that you never forget. The second when I was thirty. None since then."

Instead of speaking, Ryder tilted his glass to Kai.

Kai nudged Jess with his hip. "What about you? Ever been in love?"

She shook her head. "Nope. Not the forever kind. My last serious relationship was with one of Ally Wilson's friends. His name was—is—Craig. That's how I met her. We're on good terms now. He's a friend."

Ryder grunted, and his shoulders rose and then slumped as he exhaled, like his burden was never far away. Jess had always been aware that the singer had something dark in his past, but wasn't close enough to him to be in his private circle.

"I hope me and Jess' tryst doesn't concern you, does it? You don't strike me as the possessive type."

Kai's jaw tightened before he relaxed it and took in a deep breath. "You'd be surprised. I would say no, but I've been behaving contrary to that. However, the truth is that as long as the relationship is settled, the fact of it isn't a concern. The present is what matters. We all have pasts. Nobody gets out of childhood without scars."

Kai Halara was one of the most confusing men in the world. She had to run. She had to wrap her body around him and kiss him until neither one could breathe.

"You haven't exactly showed that." She hoped her voice was steady.

"You're right. I'm working on that." He turned to

Ryder. "What about you? Have you been in love?"

Ryder poured himself a shot, studying the bottle before holding it out to them. Both Kai and Jess shook their heads.

"There's only one woman for me, but it's been over for a long time. I have no expectation things could change." Ryder studied his glass and then stared out the window.

The flash of highway lights had never been so miserable. Like her, Ryder was made of secrets and pain.

"Is she dead?" Kai's question hung in the air, the stark words their own rhythm.

Ryder swallowed and made a negative gesture, the movement jerky. "No."

"Then there's hope."

Ryder pressed his lips together, his shoulders slumping. The sensation of Kai's arm brushing over hers sent tendrils of desire through her. She'd had lovers, but she'd never longed to be consumed by one person. Until now—and Kai.

"Nah. I lied to her and betrayed her the way nobody should. We were each other's first loves, and that made the deceit worse. Some things can't be forgiven." He gestured to the bottle. "Today is the anniversary of our first meeting, all those years ago. I was playing a tiny club, and she came with friends. Thanks for coming on board. I couldn't bear to be alone. I'm already ready to crawl inside this thing. It would have been unbearable without company. I appreciate both of you."

"You do yourself a disservice," Kai said, his voice quiet in the sudden hush of the cabin. "Her as well."

"I don't understand what you're getting at." Ryder reached for the bottle and then shook his head.

"Has she ever gotten married?"

"As far as I can determine, Eve is still single. I don't ask, though, so anything is possible. Her folks hate me, so even if she was, they wouldn't tell me. I have no idea who her friends are."

It dawned on Jess that Ryder must have checked this mysterious "Eve's" social media. Something so unexpected in a man like Ryder made her like him even better.

Kai leaned forward. "Soulmates come around once in a lifetime—if you're lucky. If you found that missing half of you, do everything in your power to make it right." He shifted to align their bodies until their legs were pressed together and their torsos met.

She didn't understand what was causing this change in attitude, but was going to enjoy it while it lasted.

"It's funny," Ryder mused, tracing the rim of his shot glass with his index finger. "I told Ally something similar. Guess I'm good at giving advice but not taking it." He studied the whiskey bottle but shook his head. "I've had too much to drink." He lurched to his feet and swayed.

Jess extricated herself from Kai's grip and moved to hug Ryder. The singer threw his arms around her and held her close, his hands clenching on her back.

****

Having the woman he desired in the arms of her former lover sent a bolt of primitive jealousy down his spine.

She'd called him unreadable and impassive. If Jess could have glimpsed what emotions were roiling under the surface, she would never call him that again.

Ryder shook his head and stepped back from Jess.

"This fool is going to bed. Take any of the bunks—I've got plenty. Or share. I'll see you in the morning."

It wouldn't be the same as burying himself inside her body, but holding her would be a solace of sorts. "Good idea." Kai's voice was gruff and low.

Ryder gave them a quick nod and headed for the bathroom at the back of the bus.

"You think so? For us..." Jessica gestured to the bunk she'd dumped her blanket and pillow on.

"Is it wise?" he asked. "Maybe not. But let's do it anyway. I'd love to spoon with you and hold you until both of us fell asleep. It would make me feel..."

Virile. A real man. A stud.

He was losing his mind.

The bus jerked as it turned onto the 405 and began the journey to their next destination—a resort about an hour south of Sacramento.

Kai took her hands. The calluses on her fingers and palms reminded him that she was a musician. He'd been around so many that he tended to lump them into the same category. Flaky. Unreliable. Unsteady. But that wasn't true of Jess.

"Kai, you are confusing the hell out of me."

He was thirty-five years old and had never been more muddled in his life. He couldn't imagine what Jess must be experiencing. "Would it help to be told I am jumbled too?"

Jessica flexed their joined extremities. "You're older and are supposed to be wiser." Her expression shifted like she was trying to find the right words to convey what she meant, but came up blank. "I'm not going to say no, Kai. But you're making me crazy."

Me too.

Ryder emerged from the bathroom, clad in sweatpants and a UT Longhorns T-shirt that was stretched and faded. He grinned at the pair and went to his bunk. "Night, you two. Thanks for the company." He slid under his blanket, rolled on his side, put his cheek on the pillow, and threw his arm over his head. Within a minute he was snoring.

Kai chuckled, shaking his head.

"Ryder's like that," Jess whispered. "He falls asleep at the drop of a hat."

"Jess…"

"Sorry."

He grazed her lips with his and let her go. "Wash up. I'll change out here, and then we can get some sleep."

When she came out, her face was scrubbed clean of makeup and her hair back in a ponytail. His fingers curled under the blanket as he fought to control the desire—the need—to claim her for his own. This almost shy woman was the real Jessica Baker, with no artifice and no pretense. Every inch of him yearned to haul her to him until the world narrowed down to the two of them. The only ones that mattered.

"Come spoon." He was on his side, one arm over his head and the free hand holding the blankets of their now shared bunk.

She did as he requested, fitting her back to his chest. Her body nestling with his made Kai take several breaths before he trusted himself to let the blankets fall across their shared space.

"You are so warm," she murmured. "Do you have an electric blanket under your skin?"

If his laugh was strangled, he hoped she would be discreet enough not to mention it. She had to detect his heavy arousal even though he was trying to keep some distance. The heat of his skin had nothing to do with electricity. Not the created kind. This one was all about the proximity of a certain singer and his intense reaction to her presence.

"You are heaven and fire and all good things. Rest, Jess." He pressed a kiss on the crown of her head.

As Kai drifted off to sleep with his arms full of this captivating woman, he tried not to think about the predicament he was in.

If he did what he had been asked to do, she could lose the progress that she'd fought so hard to build.

If he did not, then he wasn't fulfilling the verbal agreement he'd made with Gordon. At this point in his life, he had nothing but his reputation to sustain him. The potential opportunity at Plausive might evaporate if word got out that he couldn't be trusted with the tough stuff. These sorts of decisions were never easy, but they were part of the job.

He'd dealt with artists throughout his career, and Jessica was no different.

Yet she was. He tightened his arm around her, and she gave a sigh that suggested she wasn't asleep. He longed to do more than glory in the tendrils of her silken hair and the warmth of her skin on his. He could so easily take advantage of her trusting body curved into his and kiss her until she was breathless under him.

Once he did, he doubted he could stop. He was pretty sure she wouldn't ask him to, Ryder or no Ryder. Heat surged through his bloodstream as he inhaled her floral scent.

She wasn't anything he'd expected. She had depth and honesty, and everything inside him told him that this woman was older than her years. That phrase was too often bandied around like a cliché but, in Jess' case, nothing but the truth. Kai forced himself to quit thinking about all the ways that she was different.

He couldn't go there and stay focused on what he had to do. He was committed to a course of action, and he was honor bound to finish the task.

Whether he wanted to or not.

Chapter Eight

Jess walked down the steps of Ryder's bus, shading her eyes with her hand to ward off the morning sun. She stepped into the gravel of the parking lot, glancing at her surroundings. All around her was greenery, lush trees, and bushes leading up a steep hill. To her left and down was a large, sparkling lake that was one of the attractions of this place. Boats and bathers were already in the water, despite the early hour. The resort had an anticipatory aura, like the buildings were waiting to catch up to the promise of the day. The rooms, more like apartments than a hotel, were stacked farther up, the ones facing the lake affording an excellent view of their surroundings.

No doubt she'd be in a room on the far side. The owners would save the best accommodations for paying customers, not the entertainment.

Ryder might be the difference between a foundering career and a successful one. With the mediocre returns her album had garnered, she was in a tenuous position. Jess had spent too many years living in reality not to understand what continued failure could mean for her future at the label. All she could do was keep going. She was a survivor. If Shatter Sound walked away from her, she would find a way to get through it.

She always did.

Jess shook her head to rid herself of her musings and started for her idling bus. She stopped when Kai emerged from Ryder's bus, Ryder close behind. They were engaged in an intense conversation.

She would give anything to learn what they were talking about.

As she watched, Ryder whispered something to Kai, then stepped back and retreated inside.

Kai caught up to her, and they headed for the lodge to check in. They walked in silence, something she was getting used to around him. He didn't fill the air with words just to hear the sound of his own voice.

"What did Ryder say to you?"

Despite the hour, several guests were already waiting ahead of them when she and Kai went inside. She got in at the back of the queue, aware that he was behind her—and he hadn't answered her.

"It's a beautiful day. Once we get checked in, we could get food, if you're hungry."

She pushed at his chest when they inched forward. "You're dodging the question. What did Ryder say to you?"

He hesitated and shook his head. "Male/male privilege. No girls allowed. It's a guy thing."

She snorted, an inelegant sound that echoed through the open area. "Right, because that's you. Football games, belching, and racing monster trucks. What did Ryder say?"

"You're a bulldog."

She peeked up at him. "I'm persistent."

He grunted out something that might have been a laugh before his face shifted to a serious look. "He said you're one of the most complex humans he ever met and even though you two were friendly, but not friends—yet—he had the utmost respect for you. He considers you to be a friend. I get the impression that despite the fact that Ryder has a lot of sycophants around him, he has few people he can trust. He said he wasn't sure what was going on between us but that you were a keeper. I need to hang on to you and not let you go."

"I always liked Ryder. You should listen to him."

Kai's face went serious, the stillness she'd come to associate with him manifesting. "I have many reasons why my brain tells me to disagree with the man. Among what we've already discussed, you and I are in different places in our lives. I have no business getting involved with you."

Jess tried not to let her sinking spirits show on her face. She might have stammered something before she focused on the floor.

Then he touched her cheek, some of the humor coming back into his face. "Then again, maybe I should."

She opened her mouth to say something when the line moved, and she shuffled forward to the check-in desk. Then she was absorbed with the particulars, most of which had been handled by Rick prior to their arrival. The clerk handed her a large room key, and she pushed to the side.

As Kai took her place and gave his name, Jess' cell phone rang.

She'd set her ringtone to "warning, warning, warning" a dozen years ago to alert her about who was calling. The words were as loud in the room as her snort had been earlier. She caught some guests glancing her way and silenced the ringer. The screen flashed back to her home picture and then started again.

She searched for something to distract her, but Kai was in an animated discussion with the desk clerk. Her device went dark and then lit up again.

Her parents would call until she relented. She was aware that responding was a dumb idea—her therapist had told her that—but she couldn't quite shake the habit. Jess found a quiet area just outside the lobby, near an empty ATM. She took several deep breaths to calm herself before swiping left to accept. "Hello?"

"Jessica, it's your father." His voice was jovial and too loud.

She leaned on the back of the terminal. She should never have answered. She had done this dance a thousand times, and the outcome was the same. She had more awareness now than to be taken in by their so-called emergencies. She was smarter than this.

"Hi." She kept her tone neutral, neither welcoming nor hostile. Either led to uninvited attention.

"How's my peach?"

"I'm fine. What's up?"

Her dad huffed. The manipulative sound was far too familiar, yet she couldn't help the surge of guilt at her brusque words.

"Can't I call my girl to say hi and find out where she is and what she's up to? You're on tour with some fancy country guy—at least that's what the neighbors said."

"We're in a resort south of Sacramento. And no, you don't." Her voice was strangled and a half octave higher than usual. She struggled to visualize calm, taking deep breaths to quell her surging panic. Whatever they were going to ask her for, she had to say no. The ingrained habits of a lifetime flooded her. She had to end the call and run for her life.

Somewhere. Anywhere.

Her dad didn't say anything for a minute. As she

waited, Kai turned away from the desk as the clerk pushed back, polite dismissal written on his face. Kai started to say something, but then he shook his head and walked from the counter.

He headed in her direction but stopped when Jess held up her hand.

She pointed to the phone. "My parents." She mouthed the words, and he grunted, folding his arms.

Her father's shrill syllables caught her attention again. "We've gotten into a fix."

Her shoulders hunched, and Kai's focus fixed on her at the subtle movement. He was much too observant.

"What now, Dad?" Whatever her father was about to say, she doubted he was speaking the truth.

"We, uh, owe back taxes, and they're going to take the house if we can't come up with a thousand dollars." He sounded unnatural, a rising cadence that was all too familiar. It told her everything she needed to know about truth—and lies.

The reality could have been any number of things. They could have borrowed money from friends for "bills" when their funds ran low and now had to pay it back. Or even gotten a loan, though that was unlikely. Whatever the actual situation was, Jess would never be sure. Their credit history was a wasteland of collections and bankruptcies.

"I don't have that kind of ready cash."

Kai tilted his head to study her.

"C'mon." The wheedling left her dad's tone to be replaced by a hint of anger or impatience. "You're a famous singer. You've got to have a thousand bucks."

"Shatter Sound Records gave me an advance to make the album. All the profits I make are paid back to them until that is settled. I'm not rolling in available cash."

A memory caught Jess of a time she'd tried to enter a singing contest when she was ten. Her parents refused to give her the admission fee. When Rocky got wind of their actions, he'd taken care of the cost and a ride. It had been the first time but wasn't the last. Rocky had saved her more than once when her relatives failed, if he was aware of what was happening. As she got older, she'd kept her trauma to herself as much as she could. Her brother had his own life to lead and didn't need to be bailing out his kid sister, the one he'd left when she was eight.

"You're on the country charts. You have to be rolling in dollar bills."

She wished she could hand the phone to Kai to have the former label president explain the reality of the record business. But this was her family, her problem. He couldn't help her. Over the years she'd learned that nobody would. Just her and her alone.

"Recoupable advance, Dad. That means the company that signed you fronts what's needed and you pay it back off the proceeds. If any. You don't make a profit off your first record unless it explodes. My song isn't doing great, far from that high bar. I don't have it. I'm sorry."

"We'll lose the house."

Jess sighed. The chances of her father telling the truth were slim, but she needed to make sure. "I'll call you back." She hung up, ignoring her father's sputtering protests.

Kai opened his mouth to speak, but she put her hand on his arm, forestalling his words.

"Wait."

He subsided, retreating into his normal straight-backed stance, watching her.

The phone rang once, twice, and then a familiar female voice answered. "Aunt Jess! I heard the landline and figured some dumb guy was trying to sell us siding, but it's you. Yay."

"Hi to my favorite niece. I wasn't sure what anyone's schedule was and, as it's before work hours, supposed this was my best shot at getting someone. How are you? How's school?"

Jess listened while her teenage niece launched into a detailed description of her classes and her companions, as well as homework. She started to describe her extracurricular activities when Jess cut in.

"Van, I want to hear all about it, but I've got a sort of emergency. Can it keep? I need to talk to my brother. Is he around?"

"He's already at the office. Had to go in for some meeting, I think. I wasn't paying attention, but I think they had to call overseas and needed everyone there. He's home half the time, but you missed him today. When are you coming here?"

"Ah. I should have called his cell. I hoped to catch him here, eating breakfast or something." Jess met Kai's gaze again, and the flicker of sympathy made emotion race through her. Hope joined the dread and concern curling around her spine.

"He might be done by now. You can try."

She wasn't sure what day it was. Today could be Tuesday or Friday or the middle of next week. She lost track of the days on the road. One tended to blend into the next. "Thanks. I'll call him there. As for when I can visit, maybe after this tour. But I might have to go back into the studio. It's hard to say. Give my best to your mom."

Kai stayed quiet as she punched in a new number. She could tell he was puzzled, but he said nothing.

"Rocky here. Is that my famous sister on the line?"

"You got it, Rocky. It's Jess."

A long, heavy sigh on the other end gave her all the information she needed.

"They called you too." Her brother made the words a statement, not a question. "That's why you're calling. Not that I am unhappy to hear from you, but…damn it."

"Yeah." She noted that Kai had done that impassive thing with his face again, his arms folded. "Is there any truth to it?"

"No way. I told Dad to give me the account and address information and I'd pay it online, and he refused. He said we should just send him the money."

"What do you think it's for? Booze?"

"It makes no difference why they are asking. He's not getting a dime from me—and he shouldn't get any from you."

Jess sighed, similar to how her brother had a short time ago. "You're right. It's just hard to say no."

"Do it. Stay strong. I've got your back. Whatever you need, say the word, and I will do it. If you are about to cave, call me and I'll remind you why it's a bad idea. Now for the fun stuff. When are you going to come visit? Is your tour taking you our way?"

She grinned. "It's not, but I'll work something out. As I told Vanessa, I might have free time when this is done. She's thirteen going on thirty, I swear. Thanks for the info. I have to go. Talk to you soon."

She flipped the phone closed. It rang again at once, and she pressed ignore.

"I assume that was your brother?"

Kai's voice came from a distance as she watched the screen go black and then start again.

"That's right. Rockwell is his legal name, but he's Rocky to me. He lives north of here with his wife and teenage daughter."

He uncrossed his arms, his posture loosening. "He's young to have a teenager."

"Not really. Rocky is ten years older than me. He moved out when I was eight and him eighteen. He had good reasons, though he hated leaving me…there."

His lips turned down. "You say so much without revealing anything specific about your past."

Her phone lit up again, and Jess again pressed ignore, words jumbling inside her. "Kai…"

He shook his head and gestured to her mobile. "Turn it off. Why don't we go down to the lake and put our feet in the water? You can tell me about your family."

The idea of revealing her truths to Kai made Jess shiver. She'd read that men should check out the mothers of the women they were involved with before they would consider a lasting commitment. Her mother and father would make any sane man run screaming. They already had. If they'd been different, perhaps Craig wouldn't have dumped her. The reasons, if not the man, haunted her.

Not that permanence was a possibility. Even if they got involved on some level, Kai wasn't relationship oriented. At least, with her—a too young musician. Maybe if she was a nice, astute brunette with sharp cheekbones and mysterious ways, he might change his mind. And if she was between thirty and thirty-five, that would be ideal. She had nothing to hold a man like him.

Her therapist would say that this was an old tape playing. The woman believed in Jess more than she did. But she wasn't wrong, and Jess was aware of her own self-sabotage. She had as much to offer as any woman. This ridiculous internal dialogue running herself down had to stop.

"Don't you want to put your clothes away before they wrinkle? Or is it too late for that?"

Kai waved it off. "Later."

His words were clipped, and something in his tone made Jess pause. But then he took her arm, and the rest of the world faded. Perhaps she could show up at his room with a bottle of wine and… She tucked those delicious fantasies away for a later date.

She had to enjoy this time with Kai and not expect more. To do anything different was just leading to more trouble.

Maybe she would figure out what room he was staying in anyway.

Jess hugged the idea to her as they headed for the lake.

Chapter Nine

Kai took his shoes off. Jess followed suit, aligning her sneakers and folding and laying her socks on top. He dangled his feet in the water and gave her a gesture to do the same. His jeans were pushed up over his calves, and she caught a glimpse of well-defined muscles. His presence was all around her, stimulating and somehow comforting at the same time.

They watched the glint of lake and hill mingled together, the sun gleaming off the waves.

"It's beautiful here," Jess said. "What a terrific place to have a gig. The scenery is out of this world."

Kai gestured to the lake, his sweeping motion one of silent assent. "I'm surprised you've never been here before. My artists were too hard rock for their booking agent, but I've been aware of this location for a while."

"I don't pull in the kind of crowd that would attract the attention of this place. All of this is due to Ryder liking me enough to get me on the tour."

She realized her mistake when he stiffened.

"You get what I mean. We were both in that bus last night, right?" She tried to meet his gaze, but he shifted away from her. "I can't apologize for what happened between me and Ryder again. It's getting old, and you said you understood. It would be great if you acted the way you said you felt."

She moved to stand up, but he enclosed her hand in

his, holding her still.

He gazed across the sparkling blue of the lake and to the mountain beyond. "I'm sorry, Jessica. I'm not a jealous man. But with you all those rules go out the window. I can't abide it when men flirt with you, though I recognize that's how things are with musicians. I don't have a clue what happens next. Perhaps nothing. But despite myself, I can't help but be drawn to you—in every way."

She leaned in and put her cheek on his shoulder. She could smell the faint scent of his aftershave and the lingering residue of soap on his skin. His hand was warm and strong, caressing her upper arm as he held her to him. The roar of the motorboats echoed across her ears before Kai's presence blotted out their existence.

"Now tell me the story about your parents. It must be quite a tale for you to write the songs you have and have the ringtone you do. Not that I can blame you. Anyone who would blow up your phone like that has issues."

Jess stared out over the water, his warm hand curled around hers. "It's not pretty."

"Families rarely are."

She filtered through all the stories in her mind, trying to decide how to begin. "My dream has been to be a musician since I was old enough to walk. You must have encountered many like that when you ran the label."

"Sure."

That simple word gave her strength. She took a shuddering breath and continued. "My parents had CDs in the living room—product of their time. I think maybe once upon a time one of them was into music before the addiction took hold. Rocky, of course, preferred his devices, but he listened to the CDs too. We had a lot of grunge, like Nirvana and Pearl Jam, and they were okay, but I preferred Van Halen and Guns N' Roses. I liked guys like Johnny Cash, Travis Tritt, and Dwight Yoakum even more. Country music spoke to me—I related to the undercurrents. Rocky left a guitar behind when he escaped the house. He said I could have it. I picked it up one day when…well, nobody was watching me. I was nine perhaps, or maybe ten. The guitar was too big for me, but I persisted despite that. We didn't have money for anything else—at least disposable income my parents would spend on an instrument my size."

Kai squeezed her hand. "I would love to see pictures of you at that age."

She gave him a brief smile. "Rocky might have some. When I call this weekend, I'll ask him. He's a computer fiend, so if he does, he's digitized them." She followed the path of a boater as they made their way across the sparkling lake.

"Go on." His voice was gentle. "Tell me as much as you're comfortable with."

"My parents are alcoholics, but I think you figured that out already." Jess watched the waves reach the edge and roll to them. "From what I can determine, they slid into it over time, so Rocky had a normal childhood, at least the first part of it. That changed after I was born. Mom used to blame me, saying they didn't ask to have me and my coming along so late had ruined their lives. Of course she'd never remember her words in the morning. So she claimed."

Kai's voice cut into the memories that threatened to surge through her. "Addicts often project their flaws onto their family members when they can't face the truth.

Rocky was old enough, but you needed to be taken care of."

"Right. I learned all about broken family dynamics when I went to support groups and later to therapy. They taught me about parentification and narcissists…all expressions I had no name for when I was twelve."

"Rocky didn't stay? To protect you?"

When she met his gaze, compassion mixed with dark anger knitted his brows.

"He didn't—he couldn't for his own sake. Though he was spared their insanity as a kid, by the time he was eighteen, things were bad. He had to get out in order to save himself. I don't blame my brother. He did what he could. When he was there, they would steal his money, try to get into his bank, all sorts of crazy."

Kai squeezed her hand, and she clung to the contact like a lifeline.

"I don't understand all the nuances, but that will come in time. I'm interrupting."

Nobody ever cared about this part. To them, she didn't have it rough. Maybe she wasn't the superstar she'd imagined she would be, but she was still signed to a record label and had achieved success many dreamed of. She was a golden girl, a favored child, living on easy street within walking distance of the American Dream.

"My dad had gotten an inheritance when his father died. It gave them enough to live on and indulge their drinking, but not to help a child grow up." She had to get through the story without becoming too emotional. "I have had to fend for myself since I was eight years old—after Rocky moved out."

She didn't care to talk anymore. She needed his full lips on hers until neither one of them could breathe.

"Finish, Jess. I have to hear this all the way through."

She leaned her body to his and began speaking again. "It's amazing how resourceful kids can be when they have to be. I learned how to cook. Simple stuff, but it worked. I figured out how to get my parents into bed when I found them passed out on the living room floor. Rocky helped me if he happened to be there."

Kai's grip closed around her. "Oh Jess." He breathed out and then tightened his hands in hers. "You should never have had to go through that."

"Why not me? I'm nothing special. I'm just a blonde-haired brown-eyed singer in a sea of similar women trying to make it in one of the most competitive markets out there. Trust me, Kai. This isn't stuff the general public wants to hear."

"Jessica." He tucked a wayward strand of hair behind her ear. "Your parents don't define you. They are part of your history, and that is all. Their flaws are theirs, and you shouldn't take them on."

Her breath left her in a heated rush. "You'd have to meet them to understand. When I make the mistake of introducing them to a man, they never get through the night without asking my dates for money. I stopped being so foolish after the last guy. Their antics ended it, and I finally learned. They are…awful."

His dark gaze held so much sympathy Jess couldn't bear it. She blinked and coughed.

"None of this defines you. Jessica, don't underestimate your worth. Ever."

"Right. Well, I've been told the same thing by my therapist. I've come a long way from the twelve-year-old who begged her mother and father not to get trashed and go to a movie on Friday night, but that little girl still lives inside me."

"She always will. She defines who you were but not who you are."

She breathed out and back in, taking him in like the fragrant air around her. "Enough about me. What about you? You're from Hawaii, right?"

He accepted the abrupt change of topic with a nod of his head. "I am. Have you ever been there?"

"Not with my folks. We didn't travel or do outside activities—any available cash went into the liquor fund. I did go to the Big Island with a group of college friends. One of their parents had a house there. My folks grumbled about it, but I had earned the money playing covers at a local bar, and they couldn't do anything to stop me. If they could have found my money, they would have taken it—just like they did with Rocky before he left. I didn't leave anything important where they could find it. He taught me that and kept my ready cash and banking information safe at his place."

"Some should not be allowed to have children. But if they had never had you, then I never would have gotten the pleasure of meeting you. You've never visited Oahu?" At Jess' negative shake of her head, Kai continued. "The five of us grew up in a two bedroom in the interior of the island. We're hapa haole—mixed race—and not accepted on either side. They were against my parents' marriage. We lived on welfare and money from the occasional jobs my parents could get. All of us kids worked when we got old enough, which helped. I was smart and had choices when it came to college. I was offered full scholarships to three different schools. I didn't think I'd fit in at Georgia or Wisconsin, so I chose

California. I'll tell you the rest some other time. Today isn't about me. Jess…"

He put his free hand on her cheek and leaned in so close his breath heated her skin. Her vision blurred as he moved closer, and any second now, they were going to kiss. Her pulse sped up, and she turned her face to his.

Kissing him wouldn't be enough, but it would be a start. An appetizer.

Her shouted name broke into their reverie. Jess drew back from the temptation that was Kai Halara and fumbled for her phone. When she turned it on, it vibrated in her hand. She breathed out in relief when she noted Rick's number and not her parents' again, though she had ten missed calls.

"I'm monopolizing you," Kai said.

"I don't mind," she replied even as she answered Rick's call. "There's nobody I'd rather be with."

Rick was talking, and she had to leave Kai's compelling presence so she could concentrate on her road manager's words.

"Is Kai with you? I need to talk to him."

Jess handed Kai the device. "Rick needs you."

His silken hair fell over his forehead as he listened to what was being said. Jess longed to tangle her fingers in the strands.

"It's not a problem," Kai was saying. "Rick, don't worry about it. I'm fine. Thanks for checking in. Should I get Jess back to you?"

She gave him a questioning glance when he hung up.

Folding his arms, he met her gaze, revealing nothing. "I think we've done enough introspection for one day. Would you like to get some breakfast?"

Jess forgot about the exchange until later that night. She and Kai stayed at the concert while her band members tumbled out and into the nightclub for some aftershow fun. Ryder's guitar player had given her clear signals that he would be down for some fun. She was sure if she said the word, they could connect. In the past, she might have acted on the unspoken invitation, if Kai weren't there.

She wasn't that woman anymore, not since meeting him.

Kai was watching Ryder when she joined him. He nodded to her and returned his attention to the stage. This was Kai wearing his business hat. He was concentrating on Ryder's concert. It made sense. The idea was logical. Ryder was an amazing performer, and Kai could pick up ideas from him.

She wished Kai were focused on her.

****

The '70s and '80s rock influence was evident in Ryder's performance. The singer moved around the stage like he owned it, flirting with the fans and pointing out the back of the room and waving, though Kai was aware nobody could see anything beyond the first few feet. The way Ryder did it, everyone in that room must have imagined he was singing to them.

Such was the power of a true performer. Jessica was learning but wasn't there yet. She would be in time, Kai was sure.

At her prompt, Jessica and Kai exited into the corridor leading back to the resort. He waited until they had cleared the din of the concert before popping his earplugs out of his ears.

She did the same, putting her custom earplugs into a

case after removing them. "I've got to get to the merch table. I won't have many fans right now, but on the off chance somebody spent good money on a Jessica Baker ticket, I'll be there. You can stay here if you'd rather watch Ryder."

He shook his head. "I'll come with you. Ryder is very good at what he does and doesn't need my advice. He's remarkable. Few have his ability to command a room."

"That's what makes him special. I learn from those like him every time I get up there."

Her words reminded Kai of what Gordon had sent him to do. The reality of that task weighed on him like a burden he couldn't put down.

It's business and that's all. He could hear Gordon's admonition in his mind.

This wasn't business for Jess. This was her life. The truth of his dilemma stared up at him with brown eyes.

"You will get there. I am sure if you had met Ryder when he was starting out in local clubs, he would have not been anywhere near the polished performer he is now."

"Ryder had time. Things are different today."

Kai couldn't deny that was true. "Part of my downfall with Apposite was hanging on to artists for too long. I hated to give up on bands that were good. In the end, it cost us everything."

They entered the main lobby of the resort, which was quiet and, except for the check-in clerk, empty. Her merchandise table was to the side of the entrance. Ryder's, of course, was more prominent. The area wasn't that populated but would be when Ryder's concert was done.

"Excuse me, are you—I'm sorry, but I don't remember your name. The opening act."

As Kai watched, Jess summoned the most dazzling smile in her repertoire for the speaker. He wished she saved that one for him alone.

"I am. I'm about to get set up for signing autographs, but did you have something for me to sign?"

A man of about forty stood there while the woman he was with got her ticket signed. They went on their way after a selfie where all three mugged with abandon.

Jess and Kai made their way to the table, and she took a seat behind it. Tony nodded at them and handed her a pen.

His Jessica Baker T-shirt was packed, and for a mad instant Kai wished he had worn it. He shouldn't be touching the real woman, but he could rest tonight with her name on his chest.

He tried not to think about where he would sleep. The issue had not been resolved, but that didn't matter.

Some stragglers came to her merchandise area and asked Jessica to sign various items, but none bought anything. He noted she didn't push her own stuff, as any artist in her precarious position might have done. She needed to work on marketing herself. Good artists were hustlers as well as performers in the modern age.

This weakness he might be able to help with.

Ryder's set ended, and the population in the lobby exploded. Kai stayed to the side, watching as she started to get some buyers. Jess signed everything with a willing air, though she had to be tired. She'd toweled off, but he was confident she would love a shower and some sleep. The lines for Ryder's table stretched through the lobby, but Jess' were more meager.

His heart ached for her. She didn't have time to grow with Shatter Sound. Gordon would ask his opinion when they were back, but he wasn't sure that anything he said would make a difference. He was almost positive Gordon had already made up his mind. Unless Kai was wrong and something changed in a hurry, Jess was on borrowed time with Shatter Sound.

He watched until the lines diminished and the last person was gone. This time she didn't flirt with the men the way she had in Laughlin—and he was grateful for that. Tony began packing up, and she capped the pen with a weary sigh and rose.

"Kai, I think we're done here. What do you think about going back to your room for a bit?"

He stiffened. The awareness of what he hadn't told her lingered. "I need to stop at the bus. Why don't you just leave me there and go to your room? We can meet for breakfast in the morning."

He could tell that his words had been taken wrong when her expressive face fell.

She shoved the pen back at Tony and pushed away from the table. "Sure, Kai. I get it. You won't tell me what room you got in case I show up naked except for a towel. Or maybe not that. Fine. Whatever."

He watched her as she walked away, her posture stiff. He should let her go. Things would be simpler if he allowed her to misunderstand what was happening.

Instead, he followed. "Jess."

Kai quickened his pace as she dug her room key out of her bag. If he wasn't mistaken, she was about to make a run for it. They were outside now, crossing the parking lot to the path that led to the rooms.

"I can explain."

She stopped at the foot of the stairs and stayed there without moving. His soul ached at the lost quality on her face. The idea that he had put it there made his fists curl so tightly his fingers showed white.

"Leave me alone," she said when he caught up to her. "Just…let me go."

He cursed, a pungent oath that his grandfather used when he was mad. "Jess…"

She leaned on the handrail and slumped her shoulders. The weariness that etched her posture threatened to shatter him. He needed to protect her from the world, and he was the one doing the most damage.

"Just go away. I won't show up at your room, I promise."

"Damn it, I don't have one." He hadn't intended to tell her. "They messed up the reservations and didn't give me a room. Or perhaps it wasn't accidental. Whatever the cause, I don't have a place, and the resort is booked solid. Rick checked into it for me, and Shatter Sound claims they forgot to book a room for me when I got put on the tour. It's no big deal. I'll sleep on the bus."

"Kai…" She took a deep breath and seemed to reconsider whatever she'd been about to say. "Get your stuff. These suites are ridiculous. I have two double beds and a sofa in the living room. Either have to be better than a bunk smelling of diesel."

"Jessica…"

"No arguments, Mr. Halara. I promise not to take advantage of your virtue. But I won't get any sleep if you're in those shitty little bunk beds while we're basking in luxury. You may as well just agree, or you will be responsible for me not performing well tomorrow."

She gave him a determined stare until he bowed his head.

"I'll be right back." While trying not to think about the folly of what he was doing, Kai went to retrieve his belongings.

Chapter Ten

When Jess woke, the sun had started its ascent. Outside she detected the chirping of birds and a low roar of an outboard motor. Someone was getting an early start to the day.

She strained to hear any sound or movement from the adjacent room. All was quiet. Chills rushed over her body when she tossed back the covers. The more prudent thing to do would be to put on a robe or a sweatshirt for warmth instead of the pink cotton pajama bottoms and formfitting tank top that made up her nightclothes.

She didn't care to be practical.

When she padded into the living room, the couch was empty. The blanket was rumpled and bunched up on the foot of the pullout couch, but it didn't have an occupant. She glanced around before spotting the man who had haunted her dreams.

Kai was motionless, sitting cross-legged on the floor with his back to the room. His hands were resting on his knees. By his reflection in the sliding glass door, his eyes were closed and his lips were moving.

His black hair shimmered on his neck, its softness begging for her to glory in the thick strands. He was shirtless, the carved muscles of his back flexing with his rhythmic breathing.

Meditating. That's what he was doing.

She should walk out of the room and leave him to it,

but the vision of him was so potent that it stamped itself onto her memory. A light sprinkling of hair dusted his pecs. Black sweatpants rode low on his hips. His bare feet were tucked under his legs with his toes peeking out.

Jess told herself to turn away. He was engaging in something private, and all she could think about was caressing every inch of him.

As she watched, his eyes opened and locked with hers. Then his lips curved up.

Desire slammed through her at the roguish grin.

"You are so beautiful." He used his arms to lever himself up and then turned around, his breath catching. "Without makeup and your hair in disarray, you are a delight that nobody can resist."

All she could do was make a helpless sound.

The distortion of his sweatpants showed his arousal. He made no effort to hide it. She took in the bulge, her mind dancing with possibilities. A million jumbled desires crowded her mind.

"My life is a mess. I don't have a future, I don't have a job, and I sure as hell don't have anything to offer you." He closed the distance to stand in front of her. His gaze took in her face and lower, to the curve of her breasts and the indentation of her waist. "I told myself to stay away from you. We are on different paths, different trajectories for our lives. We don't make sense." His fingers caressed her shoulders, and Jess swallowed, trembling as reaction started to wash over her. "I've been awake most of the night on that couch attempting to blot out the fact that you were feet away. I even peeked in on you once. You were so pretty sprawled out, your fist curled under your chin and your hair falling behind your neck. It took every ounce of willpower not to throw myself on top of you and start kissing you."

"Kai," she whispered. "I wouldn't have said no."

He nodded, his hair waving with the motion.

She gripped his warm skin while trying to ignore the tempting rise of flesh that promised ecstasy—and more.

The sun broke free of the hill, dazzling them with rays.

Kai's arms went around her, closing on the small of her back and moving her close. "That's why I didn't. If you offered yourself to me the way you've been promising, with full knowledge of the future and you still wished to continue, I would never have had enough self-control to let you go." His voice was rough, and he was shaking. "I can't make promises, Jess, and I can't offer commitments. You deserve those things. But I don't think I can fight this attraction anymore."

She had never been in love, not the forever kind. She had never experienced heartbreak, had never wept bitter tears at losing a lover. She had believed it wasn't in her to love—that she was too broken by her past. Part of her embraced that.

She had been wrong.

"Are you saying you are after a one-night stand and that's all? I understood you weren't casual about sex." She took pride in the fact that her voice was steady. She had never known a man like Kai Halara.

His fierce curse made her start. She expected anger at her clipped words, but instead need and a kind of longing she didn't think she'd ever inspire in a man showed on his face.

"No." Behind his face was the promise of something, a dark, savage need. "I can't do a one-night stand—that won't be enough. But I can't make you promises or give you forever."

He was warning her not to expect too much from him. She would go through heartache and pain before this affair was over. The heartache was for a future day, not this one.

Jess hoped she was the only one aware of the sad edge to her thoughts. If this time was bittersweet, that was on her. When it came time to let Kai go, she would do it, and the best part of her heart would go with him.

But that day wasn't today.

"I don't believe in fairy tales." She tilted her face up in clear invitation. "I understand what you're telling me. You can't commit, and I don't expect you to. You tell me when it's time to go, and I will vanish from your life without fuss. But...not yet..." She moved her hips in counterpoint to his, and he gasped.

"Jess..." He gripped her and held her still. His chest heaved, and his fingers pressed into the soft skin right above her butt. "Oh...God...I want you."

"Then kiss me."

He covered her lips with his and then tasted the seam. Over and over again, he repeated the action, tracing their lines. Then his tongue danced inside her mouth, and she shuddered, heat searing through her from the tip of her head through to her toes.

She tried to whisper his name, but he filled her. She clung to the hard muscles of his back.

"Come here." He pushed them onto the sofa bed. He lay back and wrapped his arms around her, molding her body to his.

"Tell me you have condoms," he whispered before delving his tongue inside her ear.

She sighed and shook her head. "I didn't think I'd

need them."

To her relief he placed a kiss on her cheek and then touched his head to hers. "That's wonderful."

"You don't mind?"

"That I can't make love to you? Of course I do. But I love that you're not that casual. And we can still make out."

"That's such a high school term. I'm twenty-five, not sixteen."

"Yes, of course." He smoothed her hair back and kissed her neck, tasting her skin. "Can we?"

"Oh yeah."

Jess leaned in, and their noses bumped. Kai laughed and tilted his head before pressing his cheek to hers, the contact cool and warm at the same time. He shifted again, moving his head just enough to touch her lips. The light contact sent bursts of sensation over her skin, like fireflies settling over her body. His hard cock slid between her thighs, its fullness all she could have hoped for from this man she wanted so much. She pressed against him, every nerve ending alive where their bodies met. The imperative need to be one with him sent shivers running up and down her spine.

Kai shuddered and thrust against her again before twining their fingers together. "I need to touch your breasts. Will you let me?"

"Like you have to ask." She sat up and stripped off her tank top. Her breasts bobbed at the motion, and Kai let out a shaky moan. Jess shivered at the sound as she pushed the bra straps down and slipped free of the cups.

"Hold on." Flexing his legs, he moved to a jackknifed position, his legs bent so he was in a vee shape.

She followed his lead, her legs to either side of his body, his hard arousal pulsing between them.

"I have to see." He pushed their joined palms away from her nakedness.

Sunlight played across his face, setting him blazing with inner light. Or maybe the avid hunger on his face created the blaze. His hair fell over his neck when he put his mouth on a hardened nipple and did as he promised. He licked her.

She cried out at the sensation that shot through her like tiny bolts of lightning. She started moving, feeling him slide over her even through the cloth barriers separating them.

His muffled gasp encouraged her, and she slid over him, her skin tingling where they touched, while he suckled her.

From the streamers of ecstasy flowing to her core, she was aware she was about to come. Never before had a lover's touch inflamed her the way Kai's had. Calling out his name in a broken sob, she clutched at him, and he murmured hot, dark words in response even as he continued to suckle her body.

"Kai, oh God," she cried. Throwing her head back, she lost her grip on reality and slammed on his cock, shuddering with the intensity of a fierce climax. Then he shuddered as well. He took his mouth from her breasts and rained kisses on her skin, his breath hot and sultry. His body went rigid except for his pulsing cock. Dampness both between her thighs and her pajamas told her that he had come as well.

Jess pressed a kiss on the top of his head and held him. Kai was still breathing hard, his jaw working.

"Damn." She dropped a kiss on his nose and drew

back.

"Damn is right." He gave her a lazy grin that almost stopped her heart. "That's the best sex I've had in years." He made to move, but she kept her legs locked around him.

"Don't you dare back away now."

"I'm getting you damp." He stayed where he was.

She pushed closer, drawing her satiated form over his. "I love it. I've never had that happen before."

He ran his thumbs over her cheekbones and kissed her lids. She seared the image in her memory as she let them flutter shut to accept his touch.

"It's not how I end my meditation as a rule, but I may have to add it in." He shifted, removing her from his body. "Let's get cleaned up and cuddle for a while. Then let's get someone to take us to that store down the road. We need condoms."

Fortunately for them, the gift shop in the main lodge carried what they needed. Jess pretended to examine the sweatshirts as Kai purchased the condoms, adding a shot glass, a silver-and-marcasite ring, a bottle of white wine, and two bottles of soda to the order.

Ryder entered the store as Kai's purchases were being wrapped up. He approached the pair even as they heard squeals from outside. Ryder offered Kai a handshake, his expression troubled.

"I understand you had room issues, Kai. I can have my guys sort it out. You should have said something yesterday. I don't like when things aren't taken care of properly."

Kai blew out a breath. They hadn't said anything about what happened—and what might happen. The facts about why he was there, and what it all meant, hadn't escaped her. Kai might be instrumental regarding her future at Shatter Sound, and an unkind person could say she was doing this for mercenary reasons.

That unkind person, the one who sounded like herself, could go to hell.

"It's fine, Ryder. Thank you for offering, but I can manage."

To his credit, Ryder's snicker was the sole comment to Kai's words. "We've all been in flux at one time. You change your mind, text me. I'll get it taken care of."

"Noted."

Jess pointed to the store windows where more than one fan happened to be walking by the shop. Some showed signs of being roused in a hurry by their bed head and, in one case, the resort robe and slippers on her feet.

"You're not going to have privacy for long."

Ryder didn't shift focus, but his back tightened. "I hoped the hour was too early. Guess not. I should have waited. Too late now. I just came for a couple of things."

Jess gauged the attention of the nearest fan and then shook her head. "They're coming. Sorry, Ryder."

****

In a matter of seconds, one of the fans hovering around the shop found the courage to ask Ryder for a picture or an autograph. Kai was glad the condoms he'd acquired were at the bottom of the bag. He was aware that they had a conflict of interest, and the longer they kept this situation to themselves, the better.

His body still thrummed in the aftermath of their encounter. As she and Ryder made small talk, a slow crawl of desire washed through him.

Kai moved closer to Jess. Ryder's gaze shifted to Kai and then to her. Though he said nothing, Kai doubted the closeness had gone unobserved.

The doorbell overhead chimed as a new person entered.

"I was thinking about the show tonight," Ryder was saying. "What if I gave you one more song and you could do that ballad 'Shine' from the record? It's beautiful."

Jess slid her attention to Kai. "Maybe. It's not on the charts, so it might not be the best choice. I'll take the extra time, if you're sure. I could do a cover. Fans love stuff they recognize."

Ryder shook his head. "No. That one. No covers. It's a good tune and should be your next release. It has your heart and soul in it. Jess, you underestimate your ability to craft beautiful lyrics. I'll tell my guys about the change. Doesn't matter if I have to take something out. It's done. No arguments."

Kai found he was nodding, snippets of the song playing in his mind. "I agree with Ryder. I'm not sure how the resort will react to a change in the set list. They aren't paying for Jessica Baker to sing."

Ryder gestured to the front desk. "They'll live. Leave this with me."

Jess paused and then nodded, the relief in her so palpable that Kai wondered how any man could say no to her—for anything.

"I'll ping Rick and give him the heads-up. Thanks, Ryder. That's decent of you."

He inclined his head, his gaze sliding to Kai. "We all needed a leg up at one point in our lives. Not everyone got one. If I can do that for you, I'm happy to." His attention flickered as the overhead bell chimed again.

"Hi," a petite woman in her twenties broke in, her focus on Ryder. "Remember me? I'm Bonnie. Can I have your autograph?" She held out a CD, which Kai suspected she'd bought the night before.

She didn't glance at Jess or Kai.

"We're finished. He's all yours." Jess poked at Kai, who nodded.

"Of course I do. You were in Vegas and also Laughlin. Thanks for your loyalty. Should I sign it to Bonnie or something different?" Ryder asked, taking the item from her.

As if they were just waiting for someone to make the first move, those who had been lurking descended on Ryder, coming from every direction to surround the singer. After a helpless "bye" to Jess, Ryder concentrated on the fans. Kai wasn't concerned about his fate. Ryder's tour manager would extricate him if things went bad.

"Alone at last," Kai said to Jess, gripping her shoulders and placing a kiss on her neck.

She glanced around the lobby, her head cocked. "There's a room full of folks."

"We could be naked, and nobody would notice. Ryder is a force of nature. Speaking of that, have your parents called you again?"

She took out her phone and showed him the screen. "Not since yesterday. They must have gotten what they needed. I hope Rocky didn't give them money, but he might have to get them to stop bugging me."

"Your brother is a prize. If I can help in any way, say the words."

He wished he could do more to protect her from those who would use her, but he was just part of the problem. He began to speak but fell silent when her tour manager approached them.

"There isn't anything, but thank you."

The need to act burned inside him, but he said nothing. "You're about to get taken away." Kai gestured to the person coming toward them. "I'll leave you to the new arrangements. Are we on for dinner?"

"Can't wait."

Chapter Eleven

—Come to the hot tub. I've got it going, and the wine is chilled.—

Snapping her phone shut, Jess bid a hasty farewell to the guys and headed out the back door. She began running to her suite before she forced herself to slow her steps. Behind her the strains of Ryder's first hit, "Call My Name," were accompanied by the roar of the sold-out crowd. The air smelled of jasmine and water and the earth.

At the top of the stairs, Jess stopped, her hand on the rail. Sweat covered her face and body, and she was weary, but she didn't dare take time to rinse off in case Kai changed his mind.

The bubbling of the hot tub was apparent through the open sliding door when she let herself in. He had drawn the privacy shades. The moon glinted past the shades, its quarter profile adding light to the evening.

Jess slipped out of her sweaty stage clothes and let them fall in a pile next to the couch. She paused in the darkened room, trying to summon the strength to step onto that balcony. If she lost her nerve and didn't go there, she would never forgive herself. She'd desired Kai for forever, and now was her chance.

She stepped over the sliding-door threshold. Kai's head was resting on the back of the hot tub. One hand was on the lip of the hot tub and the second around a wineglass.

He sucked his breath in when she emerged. His hair was damp, still straight even with the wetness of water. "You are so beautiful. Come. Get in. Let me pour you some wine."

She approached the hot tub, his avid gaze following her.

"Get in, Jess," he said, his voice harsh. "Or I'm going to make love to you on this balcony. Isn't Ryder above us?"

The emphasis on the words made her grin. "Ryder is still performing."

"Get in, or I will be too."

"Performing?"

He leaned forward, and she caught a glimpse of that great naked muscled chest again.

"Yes. Inside *and* performing."

Oh my.

"I want that." She climbed over the lip of the tub, and he offered her his palm for assistance.

"I do too."

As she lowered her naked form into the water, his calf tangled with hers. Wrapping his right leg over her left one, he flipped his foot over hers and rubbed their thighs together.

"Mm. That's nice."

"Have some sparkling cider. I didn't get wine, remembering what you said. The vintage was questionable anyway, but we're a captive audience. I hope I did the right thing."

The water lapped across her body, covering her to her shoulders. She took a sip of the proffered cider and gave him a grateful smile. "I don't seem to have the issue they do with drinking, but I like to be careful. Thanks for remembering."

"I remember many things."

She took another sip. "I'm glad. I... Kai, I'm nervous. You...me...I want this so much."

She wished she were some mysterious film-noir type and had the man pine over her, not the other way around. That woman would study from under lowered, manicured brows and draw him into her web with just that glare. Instead, she was gawky and obvious, like a schoolgirl. Except kids were savvier than she was.

"I want it too." He bent his head to capture her lips. He reached out and molded her to him. He lifted her without breaking the kiss and put her onto his lap, and she straddled him. He plucked the wineglass from her nerveless hand and set both on the table next to the hot tub.

She suppressed a shudder at his warm, wet skin against hers. To her surprise, his penis was soft, not erect as she had hoped.

She slid her arms around his neck. "Kai, you're not..."

He grinned, his teeth flashing white. "Aroused? Hell yes, I am. It's the water. It's hard, as it were, to keep an erection in these conditions. Can't you feel my heart? It's about to explode out of my chest."

She leaned against him and felt the frantic beat. It matched the pounding within her. Reassured, she ran her wet hands through his hair to reveal his cheekbones. "Ever since I met you, I've longed to be naked with you so much." She pressed kisses along his jaw as she spoke. "I can't believe it's happening."

He groaned at each touch of her lips. "That's

amazing. Let's stop talking and kiss instead. I need to taste you."

The hairs of his chest were individual bursts of fire on her skin. With a swoop of his head, he caught her lips again, his tongue delving inside. She followed him back, her tongue dueling with his in the ancient manner.

More. She wanted more. She had to have all of him.

He groaned, his hips moving. The room started to spin, and Jess wavered. The combination of running around stage, the heat of the water, and his body were making her lightheaded.

"Kai, we've got to leave the hot tub. I think I'm going to faint."

He rose with her still in his arms, his face tightening. Water cascaded off both of them, splashing back into the hot tub.

"Are you okay?" He set her down on the damp wood deck and scrambled out, using one arm to brace her and one to exit. She swayed, trying to get the night air to restore her senses. The room dipped, and she groaned.

"Jess?" He gripped her shoulders and steadied her, holding her in his powerful but gentle hands.

"I think I need a cool shower." To her dismay, her voice was shaky. "I'd like to wash the stage makeup off too."

He cradled her to him. He stepped over the sliding-door jamb and carried her into the bathroom.

"I should have been more aware." His words were clipped. "I might have thought through what a hot tub would do to you after a strenuous set." He flipped the switch on.

The harsh overhead light made her blink. He sat her on the toilet and started the taps.

Her reflection stared back at her in the mirror. The stage makeup was smeared, rivulets running down her face in streaks that turned her less like the gorgeous woman she'd imagined and more like a raccoon.

"In you go." Kai got her to her feet and placed her under the showerhead and then stepped in. Bracing her from behind, he held her, directing her into the current that poured over her body.

"I'm sorry, Jess," he murmured, kissing the top of her head. "When I saw the hot tub last night, all I could think about was you and me making love in it. I didn't stop to think you would be exhausted. That was selfish of me."

She stood there as the water cascaded over her, stripping the sweat and makeup from her. He supported her as she waited for the dizziness to recede.

"I was dreaming about it too." She put her hands over his and leaned back. "We should try again sometime soon."

His cock began to stir to life, hardening at the small of her back. "Yes. I'd like that. How are you?"

"Better. More like myself. Thank you."

His fingers tightened on her. "My pleasure."

He reached for something, and then the hard bar of soap touched her skin.

"I'm going to wash every inch of you." He turned her around to face him. "Then I'm going to lay you on the bed and lick what I clean. How does that sound?" The raw desire on his face made him primitive, governed by a need outside his control.

"Like heaven."

He clung to her before he released her and held the bar of soap out like a talisman. "Time to get cleaned up, beautiful woman."

He insisted on carrying her into the bedroom. Laying her down on the double bed, he hovered over her. Jess forgot about anything else when his mouth came down to hers. Kai caressed the indentation in her upper lip with his tongue until she shuddered. Then he thrust inside again, and the warmth of him filled her senses. She clutched his shoulders, drawing him close as she sucked his tongue into her mouth. His cock bobbed between them, brushing her inner thighs.

He began kissing her cheeks and neck, and she surrendered to sensation. The man she craved more than life itself was naked with her, and she couldn't have done anything else but give herself to him.

"Get ready," he said, bending his dark head until his mouth hovered just above her already hardened nipples. She thrust up, offering herself to him, and he groaned, then lowered his lips to her body.

The suction of his mouth on her nipples was wet, wonderful, and decadent. She cried out at the shock of him suckling at her and arched her back farther, letting him have full access.

****

Jess' passionate response made Kai feel like a god, a man capable of rendering the women on Earth dumbstruck. Her naked body was enough to ruin his control. He had to shift his attention away, either that or open her legs and take her, plunge into her like an animal.

He was a modern man. He could vanquish the beast.

Kai had never been so helpless when it came to sex before. The decision had always been measured, disciplined. The relationship had reached a certain point, and sex was the natural next step.

What his partners never were privy to was how much he craved that ultimate connection. Sex was great, but he had never experienced that one phenomenal cataclysm that would shift his world. That was what he craved, but it eluded him. He bent his head again and took her nipples one at a time.

Jess clutched at him at the suction of his mouth. "Oh Kai." That was all she got out before he moved down to the juncture of her thighs. Most of the women he'd been with preferred oral sex as a way to climax, and he was sure Jess wouldn't be any different. He would wait to be inside her. First, he would tend to her needs.

She shuddered at the intimate contact, clutching at his shoulders. Her legs fell open as she let him kiss her. He ran his tongue over her, tasting the wet truth of her desire.

She put her hands on either side of his face and stilled him. He was so intent on making her come he resisted for a minute, suckling on her, but then released her when she continued.

"Jess, I am dying for you to come."

She kept her palms where they were until he focused on her. The passion and desire stamped on her humbled him.

"Not unless you're inside me. You going down on me is great, but it's not the same. Please, Kai."

He reached for the condoms he'd left on the nightstand earlier that evening. When he tore a packet open, the condom fell to the covers and got buried in the folds of the blanket. With a cry of dismay, he put his hand down to try and find it, but Jess placed her hand on his arm, stilling him.

"Get a new one. I can't wait."

He fumbled over a packet resting on the dresser, and the condom flipped out with the violent motion. This time she caught it before it got lost in the bedding. She held up the condom in triumph before putting it on the tip on his penis. He jerked when she rolled it onto the remainder of him. Then she waited, her hand wrapped around his base.

"Please, Kai," she repeated.

He was sheathed and ready, but he hesitated, struck by a sudden case of nerves. Making love to Jess was something…concrete…permanent…

Too late for regrets. He opened her to him and entered her with care. She was tight and wet, her body gripping him in a welcome vise.

"Oh my God, Kai," she cried, her nails raking his back. "Oh…yes…"

He thrust into her, clutching her to him like a wild man. He tried to stop to let her adjust to him, but she was already undulating around him. She was writhing, clawing at his back, signaling her impending orgasm.

He continued to thrust inside her, his thrusts becoming wilder as his excitement built. The part of him that could still think was stunned to imagine she was coming just by his touch.

She was gripping him, her head thrown back on a series of throaty moans.

"Kai…" she cried. "Yes. Now." She jerked and moaned, thrashing on the bed, crying out his name.

He waited until her fire had cooled and then surged as passion swamped him, close to an orgasm bigger than he'd ever experienced. "Jess."

"Come for me, Kai. Please. What do you need me to do?"

He was a king. "Nothing except me taking you." He kissed her and then thrust into her, feeling her slick welcome. "Here I come."

He plunged and shouted something unintelligible. Pleasure took him, and he shouted out his desire on a cry that was her name, sinking into her like a caveman but unable to stop his actions. The tidal wave of his orgasm rocked him to his very core.

When he could think again, he focused on Jess. She ran her fingers over his back, and tiny bursts of pain erupted on his sweaty skin. She must have done that in their mutual moment of ecstasy, but he didn't recall. Nor did it matter.

"I hurt you," she whispered. "I'm sorry."

He rolled to the side. "Did you?" He took her hand and traced his tongue along the palm. "I wouldn't change a thing. Amazing." He reached over and rubbed his hand on her cheek. Her hair was wet clumps that showed the shower—and their passion. She didn't have a scrap of makeup on.

No woman had ever been more beautiful.

"That was remarkable. I've never had a woman come like that before. I've never come like that."

Confusion and desire warred within him, the truth about their shattering encounter suggesting something he wasn't ready to face. He touched her cheekbones and glided his fingers over her lips. He had to imprint this time on his mind, memorize it for future occasions.

Kai leaned back on the bed and moved her to his chest. "Let's rest for now. And then I will start all over again. I'm glad you ate your vegetables at dinner, because you're going to need all the strength you can get."

"Sounds good to me."

Often, certain words should be spoken at a time like this. But he wasn't that man, and their relationship didn't work that way. The parameters had been set—by him. They would never be any more than this, and he would be wrong to offer false hope.

She laid her head on his shoulder and fell asleep.

Kai stayed up longer, examining all the ways his life had just gotten complicated.

Chapter Twelve

Jess bent her head to the song she was working on and became absorbed in her melody. The music caught her, and she followed the notes, losing herself inside the half-formed idea dancing in her brain. Kai walked up the aisle of her bus, balancing his body at the shifting of the vehicle as it rolled along.

After a couple of minutes, she stopped strumming the guitar and yanked the headphones off. A good idea lurked in her mind, but she couldn't get to it. She was about to set her instrument aside when Kai put something in front of her.

She glanced at him and then down to the sheet of paper, which had a clef and a melody written on the chart. She began to pick out the notes written down.

"What's this?" The tune was similar to the riff she'd begun. Jess hummed to herself as she began the new arrangement.

The band was playing cards at a table in the back, paying the duo no attention as they strategized their poker game. Through it all the hum of the road as they headed for their next destination was its own song. A snippet of a Johnny Cash tune came into her mind, accompanied by the imagined sound of a train.

Kai rose to his feet. "I've been listening to you try to find the heart of this piece over the last week. It's been ages since I wrote anything, but your melody inspired me. Here's what I came up with, in case it's helpful."

Jess' fingers paused on the guitar. "I wasn't aware you were a writer too."

"If something inspires me, the muse comes. Your song called to me." He gestured to the sheet of paper. "You sight-read."

She nodded before bending to her instrument again, picking out the tune as she spoke. "Of course. I had a plan if the whole performer thing didn't pan out. If I hadn't been able to be successful as a country singer, I was going to join a touring band or do studio work or something. Rocky suggested I learn to sight-read—when I was thirteen that was my version of practical."

The bus shifted as they went around a corner, but he stayed balanced. Of course he did. That *Shotokan* he practiced gave him all sorts of powers. She wished she had some of them.

"Your brother is important in your life."

She once again stopped playing, a million words crowding her. "Yes. He taught me many things but also encouraged me to be impractical and go for my dream while hedging my bets by having a sort of backup plan."

"I love that in you." He hummed the melody under his breath and watched as Jess started playing again. "Too often I encountered artists who had crafted one good album but had no thought of what they would do next if they crashed and burned. Many of them had no alternate."

"That's me." She continued to strum the melody of the song. "Just super realistic, practical Jessica Baker. Twenty-five going on fifty. If this collapses, I'll figure something out. I haven't spent most of my advance, so I have that, if necessary."

She stood up and shoved her guitar back into its stand, then made her way to the bathroom and closed the door behind her.

Jessica studied her reflection in the mirror. Large brown eyes were reflected back at her—ones shadowed by the awareness of loving someone who didn't love her in return. She took a deep breath and squared her shoulders. The tour would be over in no time. She had no expectation that Kai would continue this affair when they were back in Los Angeles.

Satisfied that her expression was as neutral as she could manage, she emerged.

The bus had stopped, and the guys had begun unloading the gear. She started for the front to help, but Kai was there, waiting just outside the bathroom.

"Jessica." He said the single word with relief and then took her into his arms.

A femme fatale would resist him. She would stand there, glaring, until the man quailed at her anger. Then she would step out of his embrace and stare down her nose at him. He would sputter and turn various shades of red before falling to his knees to beg her forgiveness.

Jessica wrapped her arms around Kai, holding him to her.

"Jess," he said, and his voice had a helpless edge to it. "What's wrong? I like that you're levelheaded. It's not a bad thing."

He didn't love her, but that wasn't his fault. She had made a deal, and she would stick to it.

"Sorry, Kai." He couldn't help it. "Sometimes I react based on my past rather than reality. Being called practical isn't very sexy."

His fingers stilled. He pushed back from her and

clenched her shoulders. "Do you think…" He trailed off, staring at her with a combination of dismay and helplessness on his face.

The band and crew continued to unload the equipment, and she prayed that none of them would pick now to return to the bus. She made a noise and then kissed him. His lips caressed hers until she was gasping for air.

"What if I said you were the sexiest woman I'd ever met? What if I told you that just catching a glimpse of you makes me long to haul you off to a secluded spot so I could make love to you for hours? What if I told you that I can barely stand watching you onstage, so strong is my need to be inside you anytime we're together? Is that better?"

"If it's true, then yes."

He gestured down to his crotch. The hard outline of him was evident under the denim. If they'd been alone, she would have caressed him until his erect cock pulsed against her fingers.

"There's my truth. That's all that matters. All of them lust after you. It infuriates me."

The mingled voices coming their direction broke her reverie. Kai linked his hand with hers, and they made their way forward.

"They don't exist." She met his electric gaze, wishing she could rip this moment out of time and carry it with her. "The one man for me is the one I'm with right here, right now."

He let out a fast breath. "Jessica, you are amazing."

She'd take amazing. She liked that he was affected by the way others reacted to her. It didn't mean he loved her, but he wasn't unmoved. Maybe not enough for her liking, but he couldn't be indifferent. She'd spent her life living on scraps of attention, and she was used to it. She always took what she could get, whatever was offered.

Jess said nothing.

****

The man with Ally Wilson was unfamiliar to Kai but not to Jessica, judging from the way she waved and descended from the bus.

They were in Bakersfield at one of the big venues there at the last stop on this short tour. This particular location had not booked Apposite's genre of music, and Kai had never been there until now.

He'd intended to check out the venue and determine ways to improve Jess' visibility, but all his business acumen went out the window when the man gazed at Jess as she approached them like she had sunshine radiating from her.

The stranger held out his hands to Jess, and she took them. Their mutual laughs told him this was someone she had a deep familiarity with. He had assumed that she was single, but perhaps he was wrong. She didn't strike him as the type of person who would indulge in a road affair, but he might not be aware of everything about her.

Damn it.

The man had an expensive haircut, flawless skin, and a face so attractive that most women wouldn't notice Kai with him in the room. Not when this perfect specimen was standing two feet in front of them. A man Jessica had a past with.

Kai hesitated before he came forward. Jess shifted away from the man and gestured for Kai to come to them. He glanced back at the space where the band emerged, wondering if he should make excuses and retreat.

He shook his head. His behavior had no excuse. He had to do better. Kai schooled his face to reveal nothing and closed the distance to Ryder's bus. The singer was in deep conversation with Ally, his brow furrowed.

"Craig, this is Kai. Kai, Craig."

The name sent a wave of jealousy through Kai. This person was the closest Jess had gotten to being in love. The fact might have reassured Kai, since Craig and Jess were no longer an item, but he didn't care for the way the handsome man fussed over her. Though his hackles went up, Kai shook the hand of her former lover. Craig gave him a quick once-over, his nostrils flaring.

"What a nice surprise," Jess was saying as Kai stepped back from the new arrival.

Craig's grin made him even more striking. "You don't play Los Angeles anymore, Jessie. We had to drive two hours to get here, but we wouldn't miss it for anything."

Jessie. A pet name.

He was being ridiculous. She had told him time and again where she stood. Never in his life had he been jealous. Not even when he fancied himself in love. These savage, base emotions were unworthy of him.

Ally was chatting with Ryder with practiced ease, but something in her was different. She held herself with care and a hint of tragic sadness, as though she'd lost a piece of her. Kai took a beat before he recognized the thing that nagged at him. Dirk Roberts wasn't part of the group. Ally and Dirk were often together, and Kai would have believed the man would make the trip to Bakersfield with her.

"Is Dirk coming?"

Now he could not mistake the tension in her

shoulders even though she said nothing. Something had happened.

"No, he's doing something else. He's not going to be around much."

The story was not his concern. He was a hired hand, a consultant. The music industry regularly had shifts in personnel, for any number of reasons. "Got it. Who's assuming his duties? If I have questions."

When Ally spoke, her voice was rough. Kai was sure he didn't imagine the flash of pain that came and went, a shift others might miss. She reminded him of Terri in that way.

"I will or Robin. Don't worry, Kai. You'll get what you need."

He had to be content with that.

Jess' phone rang with her parents' theme, and she tensed. She shot a quick glance at Kai before Craig's chuckle broke through the sound.

"So much for them staying away. You still got that ringtone for your folks?" Craig's familiar words made Kai's teeth clench.

Jess' focus shifted to the distance as she ignored the shrill sounds. "Of course. I have to have a way to be advised not to pick up. Rocky said that he'd take care of them, and I am sure he will—or he did, and they didn't get the answer they sought."

"They didn't even leave you alone for three days." Kai considered all the things he would say to her parents if he ever met them.

Considering their circumstances, that meeting was unlikely.

The mobile went silent and started up again. Jess took it out of her bag and thumbed the ringer off. Kai noted she glanced at the screen, and the color faded from her face. She said nothing, however, dropping her phone back into the place she'd taken it from.

"Rocky is a good guy. I am sure he will take care of it if he can. You should let him. That's what big brothers are for. Are you still in low contact with them?" Craig was behaving far more like a boyfriend with intimate information of her than a person who was no longer part of her life.

Kai wondered just how close they had been and how true Jess' "almost in love" statement was. She had a past. He had a past. He would never hold that over someone. He was being ridiculous and had to correct his actions now.

"I am. That's fine for when they don't need something, but they've been bugging me over the last few days. They are after something, whether it's money or…well, money. That's all they ever ask for."

When she hadn't mentioned them again during the stay at the resort, Kai assumed they'd stopped. Or had Jess said they had? He couldn't be sure right now. "They called you again? You didn't say anything, so I believed the crisis was over for now."

Jess met his gaze, and the troubled hurt in her seared him all the way to his soul. He shouldn't have been so presumptuous. In so many things.

"No, not until now. Rocky said he'd dealt with them, but they must have not gotten what they were after, and now they're going to hound me again." She sighed and then straightened. "Don't worry about it. We have this under control."

Craig snorted and shook his head. "I remember when they once called you every five minutes for three hours—shoot, I can't even recall what incredible nonsense they were claiming. They're leeches, Jessie, and you're better off without them. You should go no contact, like Rocky recommended. Like I did. Like your therapist did. They don't deserve you."

"Can I do anything? Be of any help in any way?" Ally's voice was brittle as she spoke.

Though Kai suspected Jess would decline, he nodded to Ally Wilson. Her offer made him like the woman even more than he already did. Gordon might be ready to cut Jessica loose, but not everyone at Shatter Sound shared that sentiment. Then again, Ally had brought Jess to the label. Dumping the artist would be a black mark on her record too.

Jess shook her head. "No. This is for me to deal with. Rocky and I will handle it. We always do."

"If you say so. I can help if you need something. I've got some experience with bullies and can't stand them, even if they're related to you." Ally's hands fluttered in an indistinct series of motions. Unspoken meanings flowed under her words.

"Yeah, me too." Craig focused on Jess. "I never did tell your folks my opinion of them, but I could always do it. We got you, Jessie."

Jess' lips quivered. The adults who were supposed to protect and nurture her were assaulting her with their relentless attempts at contact. The idea of how badly they had failed her made Kai long to do something. Anything.

When she spoke, her voice shook. "Thanks, guys. I have learned not to engage. I made the mistake of picking up this time, though I just did it once. My sole recourse is to ignore them. Let it be. They will stop, in time."

Kai had to be content with that when she clamped her mouth shut so hard he could almost hear her teeth clack. He registered the faint vibration of the phone in her bag and understood they hadn't given up.

His jaw hurt with the effort not to say a hundred things—a million. *Rely on me. I can help you. Trust me. Trust us.*

The problem was the person who would do the most damage to her was himself.

Chapter Thirteen

"Jess, after sound check, let's get some food. It's been a while since I've eaten, and I'm starved." Ally had shadows engulfing her that said more than any words she might speak.

Jess didn't wonder if the absence of Dirk Roberts had anything to do with whatever was bothering the woman—she was sure it did.

Craig was there as well, a good guy with a good future. Perhaps things would have been different if she had been a less damaged woman. He was everything she should have sought, and it hadn't been enough.

She hadn't been enough. He hadn't stayed through the tough stuff. She had to rely on herself alone. Nobody else. In particular, not a dark-haired man whose life was in chaos.

"We have comp tickets at the venue for dinner," Jess protested.

"Heck with that," Craig said. "We can do better. Ally mentioned she liked barbecue when she was in Austin and she went online for local joints. Didn't you, Ally?"

No, no, no. Please don't remind Kai of Austin.

"I did. Hey, Ryder!"

The singer in question was nearby, talking to his stage manager. His head came up when Ally spoke his name, and he cocked his head at her. "Yes, ma'am?"

"We're going to get some barbecue, if Jess and Kai are willing. You're invited. There's a place called The Roundabout Bar-B-Que Pit in Bakersfield that is promising," Ally was saying. "I have no idea what it's like, but it's not too far away and is barbecue."

"I'm not eager for yet more venue food, so I'm in. Give me a half hour to finish sound check."

Ally slanted her gaze at Jess. Whatever she'd been experiencing before was buried, and all Jess got now was the capable person who worked with her at the label.

"Ally, there's a problem."

Ally tilted her head to Jess, who pointed at Kai.

"Kai's a vegetarian."

"We can go somewhere else." Ally glanced at Ryder for confirmation.

"Sure." He started to say more, but Kai raised a hand.

"I don't need my culinary needs catered to. I'm flexible. I can always find something to eat."

Jess opened her mouth to argue, but Kai's quick shake of his head deterred her.

"It's fine, Jessica. Thank you for considering me, but it's not necessary."

"I should have asked. I'm sorry."

He held up his hand. "Please don't worry. I have no issue with this."

Jess still looked as though she might protest further but then lowered her lashes. "All right then. Let's go."

The back seat of Ally's car was cramped, and Kai had to lever his long legs to the side to fit.

"Thank you." Kai's lips were by her ear, so low only Jess could hear him.

His heated breath on the sensitive skin made her

shiver. "We could have gone somewhere else, so why?"

"I don't need people to go out of their way to accommodate me. I'm already an outsider, no need to make it worse by insisting my companions cater to my culinary habits. My beliefs are my own, and I should not inflict them on those who don't share them."

"But the smell…the meat…won't that trouble you?" She had been around vegetarians before, and many of them refused to walk into such a restaurant. Or if they did go in, they spent the entire meal acting like someone had killed their best friend.

"My choice is personal to me. Don't concern yourself." He moved back and studied her. "Thank you for trying, though. For caring."

She fought the urge to lean into him. His praise warmed her more than she would admit.

The Roundabout Bar-B-Que Pit was what it sounded like, a smoky place with a handful of tables and a faint aura of Western style. Ryder's face lit up when they walked on the path to order food that was separated by a four-foot-high railing and a chalkboard with the menu selections on there.

"Yum. Good old barbecue. Can't wait." Craig held the door for Jess, and she was forced to walk ahead of Kai to accept the gesture. Craig wasn't moving until she went in first. With a puzzled glance at him, she went into the restaurant, to be followed by her ex, separating her from Kai. Craig was too close for casual contact.

He had dumped her, not the reverse, and pique that he'd been replaced had to be causing his behavior.

Kai joined her when Craig gave with ill grace, making her push past him. Kai took several long breaths, reminding her of that quiet time in her room that first day at the resort. Those heady days were so far away, though they had been a few short days or a week ago. He put a hand on her back and stroked her with his thumb. She shivered, and their gazes met.

"Thank you." He said the words for her alone.

Craig sat across from Jess and Kai after they'd gotten their meals. Ryder and Ally were on the end, talking between themselves. If anyone recognized the singer in this tiny place, they respected his privacy and kept their distance.

"So, Halara, what do you do for work?" Craig asked, waving a barbecue-sauce-coated drumstick at Kai, spilling several drops of sauce onto the plain tablecloth as he did so.

"Kai is Jess' bodyguard," Ryder said with a grin. "Does a good job, wouldn't you say? Protecting her body, that is."

Kai lowered his brows and his head until a dark aura clung to him like an ancient warrior. Jess shivered. She wouldn't be willing to cross Kai in this mood.

"I'm consulting for Shatter Sound Records at this time, but it's temporary. I'm checking into new positions, but as I'm sure you can appreciate, at my level finding the next right move is difficult. Things will work out. Why did you and Jess break up?"

Jess blinked as Craig flushed, his cheeks staining red. Kai kept his gaze on her former boyfriend, but Craig shifted, not meeting his stare.

Jess brushed her hand over Kai's thigh. He pressed his body into hers, all the while focused on the people across the table.

"Many reasons. The breakup was mutual. I needed to focus on my career. And there's…the rest."

Kai gestured to her ex, the one who had done damage to her heart, whether she had admitted it to herself at the time or not. "What do you do?"

"I'm the director of finance at an accounting firm. It's a good job with great potential. They told me I'm up for a promotion next year. Vice president, here I come. I wasn't sure about dating a musician, but, well, she's Jessie. How could I resist? That was before I learned about her folks." Craig met Jess' gaze, and then his attention went back to his plate.

Kai was almost thrumming with tension, which surprised Jess. He was the one who had set the terms of their affair, but he was acting like a jealous lover. He was out of bounds, and she would need to talk to him, but not here. Not with everyone watching.

"Craig isn't giving you the whole story. We met at a bar Craig used to go to for trivia night, and by the time we got around to talking professions on our first date, we were already interested. We tried, despite the incompatible lifestyles, and maybe we could have made a go of it, if not for my parents. They were in a manic phase at that time—like now—and kept this up repeatedly for over a week. I still had a landline back then, at their insistence. They asked for money, first from me and then from that 'highfalutin' new boyfriend.' When I shut them down, they tried to get Craig's number to call him too and badger him for the funds. They said they needed to be told where I was always. I refused, though it went against everything I'd been brought up to do, but I did it. When they stopped, I'm assuming they got what they were bugging me for. I got rid of the landline after that. Then I went no contact for a time, but the damage was done. We had no chance. I'll let Craig tell the rest. It's his story."

Kai's face fell into impassive lines and stayed there, a quiet menace radiating from him. Ally stifled what was either a gasp or a laugh, Jess couldn't be sure.

The image of snapping, snarling dogs leapt into her mind again. Kai twined their fingers together on his leg but continued to focus on Craig.

"I wouldn't like to meet you in a dark alley when you're pissed," Ryder said.

"Smart man." Kai's voice was amused.

She was going to have to research Buddhists. Weren't they supposed to practice nonconfrontation? Kai wasn't adhering to his philosophy very well.

"Guys, come on," Ally said. "We're having dinner, not throwing down the gloves for a duel at dawn."

Craig gave Ally a sheepish grin and inclined his head. "Sorry. The breakup was a hundred percent my fault. Her folks are unbelievable. Despite Jessie's efforts, they got my number and hassled me for money when she refused. I couldn't take it. I'd gotten a glimpse at the future, and it wasn't pretty." He fixed on Jess. "At the time I was doing the right thing—for me and for her."

"Her parents are not Jessica." Kai snapped out the words. "She can't help her background."

"Yeah…" Craig picked up his chicken and resumed eating. Then he put it down again. "Whether I made a mistake or not, that's the choice I went with. Jessie, how many times have they called?" He pointed to the phone face down on the table.

She turned the device over. Six calls and ten text messages displayed on the screen. Jess showed the phone to the gathering. "It's ancient history, guys. Craig and I are friends. Can you blame him? My parents are a nightmare. Nobody should have to deal with them."

Kai leaned over until his breath was hot on her ear. "None of this is your fault. Don't take it on. You had a right to a safe and secure childhood, and you were denied it."

She met his gaze, and her breathing stopped. He was leaning in so close she could kiss him if she moved. His eyes were piercing orbs, staring into her skull.

If she wasn't smart, she might think he cared more than he did. That sort of wishful nonsense got her nowhere. The evidence was seated across from her at the table.

She had to stop imagining that she and Kai were more than they were, or she was going to be in a world of hurt.

She was already too late for that.

****

Kai had been assisting in breaking down Jessica's set when the call from Dirk came in. He held up a hand to Jess and Ally, talking together backstage, and made his way outside where he could hear the conversation.

"Dirk, this is a surprise. I assumed you'd be at the show, but Ally came with a friend of hers. A man named Craig. Jessica's ex."

"Craig's an all right guy. I'm glad he can be there for her. The rest—that's a long story. Things have...changed. All of them."

Kai waited in case Dirk was going to say more, but that was all the man volunteered.

"So I understand. I'm at the venue. Jess is wrapping up. The tour is done."

Dirk swore, a colorful epithet that Kai couldn't make out. "I got the days and times mixed up. Sorry about that. It's easy to lose track of things now. If y'all need to go, say the word. This can keep."

"No. This has to be important."

"Sure is. I think so, anyway. I was on a business call with my buddy at Plausive Records, and it reminded me to check in with you. Has anyone reached out?"

Kai shook his head. "Not yet."

"They will. They are eager to get the ball rolling, and you're their leading candidate."

"That's a surprise after Apposite."

Dirk laughed. "Your label may not have made it, but that doesn't mean you didn't leave an impression. They like what you tried to do."

When he failed, he figured that was the end of that. The idea that it might not damage his career forever had never occurred to him. Once a failure, always a failure. He hadn't determined how he felt about the job at Plausive, though opportunities like that didn't come along often. He should reach out and grab the chance.

"You and I may not have had very long together before… Anyway, I liked the way you went about things. You're good." Dirk sucked in a breath, and when he spoke again, his tone was lighter. "If you took over, I'd have an even better contact, and I might need all the help I can get when my life is settled. In the past, I tossed some bands their way when Marlon wouldn't sign them. Maybe a little quid pro quo wouldn't be the worst thing."

It did not take a genius to recognize currents were swirling around Dirk—and Ally, as well as the label, and by extension, Jessica. Her well-being was what Kai was most concerned about.

He was gripping the phone too hard and forced himself to take deep breaths. "Care to tell me what's happening? I'm not blind, Dirk, and I've been in the business long enough to be aware that something is going down. If this is one more thing that is going to take its toll on Jessica, I'll be pissed. She deserves better. She's been getting short shrift all her life."

Dirk paused for a series of beats that told Kai the currents swarming over all of them had already swamped him. "I'm afraid I can't help with that, Kai. Not anymore. I can't say any more than that, not yet. Not until things settle. I'm right sorry for what I think will go down with Jessica, but it's too soon to say what could happen. The campaigns still could take hold. It may not be too late."

"Fuck. You are aware what Gordon asked me to do?"

"I wasn't born yesterday, so yeah. I can't do anything about it right now. But you can. She's good, and I would have enjoyed helping her find her right place, but nothing I can do now. It's up to you. You're a label guy and might be able to change the outcome if Gordon will listen. He sure as hell won't have anything to do with stuff I touched. It's what you were brought in to do, so nobody can gainsay it. She's a good woman and a great artist. I'm proud to have been allowed to work on her campaigns. I'm sorry...naw. I ain't going there."

"She hasn't had it easy. I'm committed to doing what I can. Thanks."

"I reckon that's all you can do. Now, about Plausive. I'll get ahold of my friend again and find out what the latest is. You don't have a contract with Shatter Sound, right? Nothing permanent?"

Kai shook his head. A text came in from Jess, wondering where he was.

"No. Just for this tour. The understanding was that

it might go longer, but that's just a verbal discussion, and as they say, that's worth the paper it's printed on. I doubt Gordon is going to be happy with what I have to say." He had been turning over ideas about how to present his ideas, but hadn't been able to find that right method. Kai was not the boss.

Part of him wasn't unhappy about that. The good thing about being a consultant was that he didn't hold artists' careers in the palm of his hand. That was also the downside. Perhaps he should find ways that he could affect lives without controlling them.

An idea danced around the edges of his awareness. Kai started to reach for it before he recognized that Dirk was still speaking. He put the still unformed notion to the side and focused on Dirk's words.

"I'll be in touch."

"Thanks. I've got to go. They're wrapped up and wondering where I am."

Dirk said nothing for several seconds. "Say howdy to…naw. Forget that. Don't say anything. Keep me posted regarding Plausive."

Then he was gone, leaving Kai staring at the phone.

The currents that he had been trying to figure out how to stave off might already have engulfed all of them. He might no longer have the ability to protect Jess from the fallout.

The idea was intolerable.

Chapter Fourteen

"We need to add some stairs to the drum risers," Kai said. "The band is energetic, and they involve Todd as they perform if we give them access."

Gordon nodded, his fingers steepled as he listened, but made no effort to write down anything Kai was saying. Ally was in the room, taking notes—and Dirk Roberts was nowhere in sight. He didn't care about the rest, just Jessica. Kai was hopeful he could change this. He had to, for Jess' sake. He'd dealt with difficult employees before, in his career and as the head of his own label. Sometimes all a person had to do was keep talking.

"She's got good chemistry with the bass player. We should have them play off that spark, maybe a little stage antics to liven things up. Also, I'd like to have more follow spots. She gets lost at times when she goes to the side of the stage."

"Duly noted." Gordon's voice was cool and dismissive. "She has no current tours scheduled, but I will file your advice where it belongs."

"I have some ideas about her persona." In the back of his mind, Kai was aware of Gordon's lack of enthusiasm but kept going. He could change this. All he had to do was keep talking. He'd done it before, with bands that needed a little more of a push.

He was going to continue, but Gordon held up his

hand.

"Thank you for your input." His voice was flat and uncaring.

"She's good and could be great." Kai pushed past the unspoken dismissal. "I think—"

Gordon cut him off. "Thanks, Kai, but that's not your role—I shouldn't need to remind you of that. I thought you understood what was expected of you, and you're giving me the opposite."

Kai stepped backward, his enthusiasm falling away by the slap of cold reality. He'd momentarily forgotten why he was there. He was a temp. He'd been brought in to seal her fate, not the reverse. Gordon had anticipated that Kai would play by the rules, and he had rebelled.

Kai had never been more grateful for his ability to school his face into impassivity. He stopped talking and stood ramrod straight, arms folded. Ally sucked in a breath at the words.

"This is my label, not yours. Jess is my artist and not yours. I get things from the road, Kai. You don't get to tell me how she should be marketed. You failed at your assigned task."

Kai took in the trembling of Gordon's body and the fine sheen of sweat along his upper lip. Anything he had to say would fall on deaf ears. Gordon had made up his mind before Kai came on. He was supposed to be a useful hatchet-man guy, not Jess' defender.

Contenting himself with a nod, Kai remained silent.

"If that's all, Robin needed to talk to you." Gordon shuffled the papers on his desk and began riffling through them.

He was being dismissed. The dismay and hint of pity Kai observed in Ally's countenance added to the despair that ran through Kai's body. He had failed at yet one more thing. Gordon wouldn't listen to him no matter what he said. Kai's time at Shatter Sound was coming to an end. He nodded and left the room.

He was aware of the signs. It wouldn't be long until Gordon released him. He had outlived his usefulness.

Ally said, "Wasn't that kind of harsh?" before his motion carried him out of earshot and the room.

A fine film of red crossed his vision, anger, fury, and hatred all warring inside. He had failed. Himself, the label—and Jess. With one more deep breath, Kai brought his roiling emotions under control and headed for Robin's office.

****

Jess didn't hear her cell ring, but the flash alerted her that she had an incoming call. When Ally Wilson's number showed on her screen, Jess swiped to accept, then took off her headphones and put Ally on speaker.

"Jess, are you there?"

"Hi, Ally," she said. "This is unexpected. What's up?"

She hadn't expected to be in contact with Ally until midweek at least, to discuss next steps. They were on sociable terms, but impromptu calls were rare.

"Gordon just reamed Kai when he tried to suggest some changes to how you're marketed. He was angry and more or less tossed Kai out of the building."

Jess' heart sank. How awful to be treated that way after everything he'd been through. "That's terrible but these days par for the course. Is there something in particular I can do about it?"

"He was pretty upset when he left Robin's office. After I saw the way you two interacted in Bakersfield, it occurred to me you might be able to reach him. Emotionally, that is."

Jess had learned where Kai lived, but she'd never visited. Their nights together had been magical, but he'd never said anything about continuing to date her.

"I'm not sure that's smart..." Jess said. "Our association is over."

Ally snorted, the sound echoing through her phone. "He was so eager to get you to the next level and had a million ideas to make that happen. Trust me. If anyone can get through to him, it's you. No matter what you guys say, or don't say, about what is happening."

"I'll head out in a couple of minutes."

Jess didn't stop to think about the madness of what she was doing on the drive to his Silverlake home. As she circled to find parking, she had time to imagine all the ways this could go wrong. She could still retreat and pretend she hadn't driven across the city to help him. She went back and forth with her internal debate. She was about to leave when a space opened up several houses away from his. Perhaps she'd been given a sign or the opportunity to make an idiot of herself.

The mid-century modern residence twinkled in the afternoon sun. Jessica paused, taking in the hills and the rush of street traffic in the distance before going to the door.

After she knocked repeatedly, the thump of a person's heavy tread on hardwood alerted her of his arrival before the door opened to reveal Kai.

He stared at her without blinking. He had on jeans, but he had unbuttoned his shirt, and it hung loose, the front open, showing an expanse of bare skin that would have been tempting under different circumstances.

"Ally told you how our meeting went." His voice was matter-of-fact and flat, with no cadence or warmth.

Jess nodded, swallowing the lump in her throat. "Can I come in?"

His mouth opened in what could have been refusal before he stepped backward, allowing her to enter.

He leaned against the door after he locked it, arms folded, saying nothing.

"I'm sorry about Gordon," she said.

He pushed back from the door and shook his head. "He had every right. I overstepped my bounds." Again, that hideous flatness to his voice.

She'd never been around him when he was like this, with all life and energy stripped from him.

Kai focused on the wall behind her instead of Jess. "I'm a temp," he continued, "and a short-term one at that. I was sent to do a job, and I failed. In Gordon's position I might have reacted the same way."

"From what I gather, Gordon was cruel. You wouldn't behave that way."

"I'm not sure you are correct. Kindness isn't always the answer." He shifted away from her, moving into the room.

Without any clear idea what to do next, Jess followed into the living room, which dominated the front of the house. A varnished oakwood floor was broken by simple area rugs, and a leather couch and black coffee table were arranged along the back wall. Over the black marble fireplace was a Japanese katana, fixed with strong ornamental brackets into the fireplace wall. A worktable with a matching chair faced out one of the front windows. The table was covered in papers, bills, and the assorted remnants of picking up life again after having been on the road. Her room was similar.

"Nice place." Any further words dried up before they were spoken. She wasn't sure what she wanted to say.

"Thanks." He laughed, a harsh, unpleasant sound. "Lucky for me the government can't take a person's primary residence, or I might be homeless as well as jobless."

She made a helpless motion and clutched her arms around her torso. She hoped he was too distracted to notice. "Kai…"

"Who the hell am I kidding, Jess? This whole thing is a farce." He gestured to his body and the area around him.

She had no clear idea what he was trying to convey.

"Gordon took me on to do the things he wouldn't. You asked, and I was a convenient fall guy. I was supposed to go with you and find reasons for him to get rid of you. He brought me on as a consultant, but he doesn't wish me to consult. He needs someone to blame when he releases you. Since I am not playing ball, I won't be around for long. My usefulness is at an end." He slammed his fists together. "I'm disposable, someone to be used and not respected. When I lost my label, I lost my identity. I don't exist." With a single, sudden movement, he grabbed his shirt and tore it from his body, the buttons of the cuffs pinging on the floor.

She stared at him as he balled the ruined item up and threw it across the room.

"I already got that, Kai. I'm not blind. Well, maybe to some things, but not that. Thank you for trying to change his mind. You're not nothing. You did what you could."

"I failed, like everything else." He gestured to the room and the hills outside in turn. "I hear the talk. *Kai Halara is a fool*. I ran my own hard rock label right into bankruptcy."

He flung his arms out, the movement causing him to lurch backward. Stumbling, he tried to regain his balance and then gave up the fight and fell to his knees. He buried his head in his hands, clutching at his hair.

Jess went to him and laid her head on his shoulder, holding him as he trembled in her embrace.

"Kai, stop it," she cried. "You are not that person." The tears began running down her cheeks, and she made no effort to check them.

"Aren't I? The industry doesn't tolerate failures. Gordon treats me the way he does because he can."

"That's insane. Don't listen to that. Your company failed. Not you. It doesn't change your worth as a human being."

"Jess…" He didn't say anything further.

"It's just not fair. This isn't right." Her tears continued to fall, rolling off her chin and onto his naked back.

"Jess, are you crying?" He sounded startled, his voice rising. "Don't. Not over me."

She pressed into him, trying to find coherency among her jumbled emotions. "I hate that you're so unhappy. You're the most fantastic man I ever met, and it's horrible that you were made to feel this way by someone like Gordon. You're twice the man he is."

"That's remarkable. Nobody has ever cried for me. You are a unique woman, Jessica Baker."

Despite the situation, she couldn't help but enjoy the heat and spicy scent of his skin. "I'm glad someone thinks so. This dream failed. Your next one won't." She wondered if she was speaking to him or to herself.

Without breaking the embrace, he took her onto his lap so her body was pressed to his. "I don't have any idea if you're right or not." Kai smoothed his hand over her hair. "But thank you." He pressed kisses on her cheeks until her tears stopped. "That which does not kill you makes you stronger." He gripped her chin and gazed at her. "I owe you a debt for reminding me that there are those who care."

Though she hadn't meant to bring up their situation, something inside Jess compelled her to speak. "We haven't talked about where we go from here."

He sighed but didn't move. "I'm aware. I still can't make any promises. Or rather, I shouldn't. It's not fair to either one of us. If you don't mind that, I'd like to continue this—whatever this is."

She stirred in the familiar heat of his presence. "Good. So do I."

He sifted his hand through her hair and ran it over her nape. Her shudder was involuntary, and she arched her neck to his hand.

He laughed, pressing a kiss to her temple. "Jess, you are the most responsive woman I ever met. I'm not up to making love."

Making love. Not having sex. The words were a small thing, but she'd take it.

She was pathetic.

"Lie back," she said.

His hand stilled, but he did as she asked and stretched out on the floor. She slid free of his body and straddled him. Running her hands over his naked chest, she kissed his navel. His involuntary grunt and shudder thrilled her. His hair spilled onto the hardwood, dark and gleaming over the oak.

"Let me pleasure you," she said, sliding over his groin.

He hardened at her touch, and his hips jerked.

"Let me do all the work."

"Jess…" Kai gasped when she ran her fingers over his hard length still covered in cloth. He moaned when she closed over him. "You don't have to."

"Of course." She moved down and pressed a kiss along the zipper of his trousers.

"Jess…" He thrust into her. "Oh…love…"

Love? More like sex. All he was experiencing was lust. Love was just a word in situations like these. She couldn't read too much into it.

She unbuckled his belt. Sliding his zipper down over his swollen length, she was careful not to hurt him. He swelled farther, and the tip of his penis emerged from his black briefs.

"I'm always hard when you're near," he said on a groan. "You're bottled sex."

She slid his clothes down and left everything in a tangle around his knees as she bent to him. She flicked her tongue over his sensitive underside, and he gasped. He held her to his erect cock. She suckled him and then ran all the way down his length. His face contorted, and he arched his neck, throwing his head back.

"Jess…changed my mind…please get on top. I have to be inside you."

She didn't have to be asked twice. She stripped off her shorts and tank top before helping him get fully naked. Then she took a condom out of its packet and rolled it onto him.

"God, your touch…" He groaned, his cock jerking when she touched him. "Take me, Jess. Take me."

She positioned herself over him. He moaned, his hips thrusting up to meet hers. She gasped at the contact as well, loving the sensation of being filled by this man.

"Jess, oh God, Jess." His fingers were trembling on her body. "I'm not going to last too long. Come with me. Please. Tell me when you're coming so we can do it together."

The sound in the room of the slap of their bodies and heavy breathing echoed around them. The pinnacle drew closer, and then she reached down and touched herself. He grabbed her breasts, rolling his thumbs over her taut nipples.

"Kai, ohh…" She threw her head back when he was all the way inside her. Streamers of passion rose in her, and she cried out to him.

"I'm coming," she said, thrashing on his body.

He gasped and went rigid. Moisture flooded her, and he pulsed, their mutual climax shattering the air around them.

As their bodies began to cool, Jess wished passion were enough.

Chapter Fifteen

He was going to have to stop this with Jess. It wasn't fair.

She was in love with him. She hadn't said the words, but the sentiment was written all over her. She watched him the same way he'd observed Terri, his former VP at Apposite, study Clarke Masters, her now husband. He would be doing both of them a kindness if he ended it.

Kai paced the conference room as he waited for Gordon. The man was already ten minutes late. Dirk should be there, but he was nowhere in sight. The official word was that he was working from home, but Kai hadn't gotten a memo or email from Dirk in weeks. He recalled their conversation in Bakersfield and could make his own assumptions. Dirk Roberts was out, and Ally Wilson was now a vice president. He'd been around the industry long enough to understand that something had happened. He wasn't privy to the details, nor did he care. Shatter Sound was a way station in his life, and people like Dirk came and went through it. Not everyone was a lifelong friend.

Kai refused to study his emotions in depth. It didn't matter what they were. This would have to end. For Jess' sake.

The initial interview with Plausive was scheduled for the next day. Kai had had several conversations with the owners over the past weeks, and though he still wasn't sure this was the direction for him, he hadn't stopped the process. He might be the leading contender for the position, provided the owner and the board of directors also were in alignment. The job was within his reach.

Short of owning his own label again, this was the second-best thing.

Kai's time with Shatter Sound was coming to an end, Plausive or no Plausive. Jess was performing in a handful of clubs over the next weeks, but he wasn't asked to go with them. His suggestions had not been acted on, and Gordon behaved like Kai had violated the employee manual. He didn't need a crystal ball to read the signs. He hadn't done his job.

He was sure Jess was doing great. All she had to do was step into a honky-tonk, and she would be surrounded by admirers dying to spend time with her, buy her drinks, kiss her…

Damn it.

He glanced at his Apposite watch. At this hour, Jess would be at sound check. He bet men were racing to fulfill her every whim. If he were there, that's what he'd be doing.

Gordon entered the room, and Kai composed his face to show nothing. The entire company was walking on eggshells. If this were his label, he would… But that wasn't fair. He hadn't told anyone except Terri about the situation at Apposite until his hand had been forced. If something was happening at Shatter Sound, Gordon didn't have to reveal it to a soul, just like Kai hadn't. His dislike of Gordon didn't change that.

"Thanks for coming." Gordon was being polite. That was a change from the last time they'd met.

"Of course. Did you need to talk about Jessica? Or was there something else in mind?"

Gordon ran a hand through his hair and then sat at the conference table. His entire body was deflated, as though someone had taken a pin to him. Kai had no idea what had happened, but the tension in the office plus Dirk's continued absence made Kai recognize whatever had gone down, and whenever it had, Gordon wasn't happy about the outcome.

Whether this was something Gordon had caused or a situation on its own, he had to deal with the aftermath. Kai again had to remind himself that this was not his concern. Not his company.

One look at Gordon's face and Kai recognized what was happening. Kai didn't need Gordon to say it. He'd been in similar situations before. He had had to do the tough stuff, and the deed was never fun.

"Kai…"

"You're letting me go."

Gordon nodded, his Adam's apple working as he swallowed. "We are rethinking our artists and going through a restructure. Jessica is part of that, but our decision regarding her is irrelevant to this situation. Your services aren't needed."

Kai rose from the table, though Gordon remained seated. A million things tumbled through Kai's mind. He no longer had a reason to be in Jess' life. This was the perfect end to their association.

Not yet. Please. I can't do it.

"That's all you need to say. You didn't make me any promises. I was brought on for a short-term assignment, and you have the right to terminate it at any point. That time is now. Gordon…" He paused. "It's not my business, but you should reconsider dropping Jessica. Her album has so many possibilities. She's a work in progress, but with proper mentoring she can get there."

Gordon shook his head. "Things have changed, and we don't have the resources to present the artists the way we had intended." Though he didn't so much as glance Ally Wilson's way, tension vibrated between the two of them. "Thanks for your opinion. I'll consider it. Robin has your final paperwork and check. She will arrange for anything you need."

Kai had to be content with that.

****

Jess watched the dancers on the floor doing a two-step while she and the band set up. They showed more eagerness for the popular song blaring from the speakers than the group opening.

In this five-hundred-person-capacity club, she wasn't even the headliner. That performer came after her, a country artist who had had several top-ten hits ten years ago and was now on the downside of the business.

Anyone who said the music business was glamorous was an idiot. Kai was living proof of that, as was the man who stayed in his tiny dressing room, refusing to come out until his showtime.

Jess shook her head to rid herself of her repetitive, intrusive, negative reveries. She was here, pursuing her dream, and that was what she needed to remind herself of. If she was smart, she would walk away from Kai and focus on her own sputtering career.

Benny stood next to her and gestured to the full club. "We're packing them in."

Few paid her any attention as she checked her guitar's tune, though a handful focused on the stage. She had her meet and greet earlier and recognized those folks in the crowd.

Jessica acknowledged the ones nearby with a wave. "One thing at a time."

Benny grimaced. "Sounds like a twelve-step thing. Or is that Kai's influence?"

She was relieved he was calling him Kai instead of new guy. She'd take what she could get.

"Perhaps a combination of both. Come on. We're about to go on." She pasted a neutral welcome on her face as the spotlight came up, checking the set list taped to the floor as she did so.

The set was a success as she counted those things. She retreated to her bus when the headliner went on. A handful of fans waited for her and the band outside. While they made small talk with the women, she signed autographs and took pictures with the diehards. She could hear the headliner, now engaging his fans where he'd been dismissive of Jess an hour earlier.

This wasn't what she'd had in mind when she dreamed of the life of a musician. She'd thought she'd write her songs and become an instant success. When Craig recommended her to Ally and Ally to Shatter Sound, she'd been ecstatic. At that time, she'd imagined that she had all she needed to make it. The truth was proving to be far less than that.

She'd get there, if she had to drag boulders over the finish line. Since this plan wasn't working, she'd come up with a new one. All she had to do was keep going.

With the fans dealt with, Jess retreated to the bus, the band following close behind. When she checked her cell phone, hoping for a message from Kai, she found none from him. She groaned and put it back down again, wincing at the notifications that were there. Three calls from her parents, but no voice mail. They must have given up leaving messages when she didn't respond to them. She was surprised they didn't text, but maybe they were already too drunk and didn't have the dexterity.

The part of Jess that was still a child contemplated calling them back, but she bit her lip and forced herself not to. She pressed her brother's number, connecting to video at the same time.

Rocky picked up right away as though he was expecting her to call. Her—or their parents.

"Hey, bro."

"Hi, Jessica. Always great to hear from you. Where are you?"

She gazed out the window and made an uncertain noise. "Some city in Arizona. It's a far cry from the tour with Ryder. What's going on? The folks have been blowing up my phone again."

"Not sure. They've been doing the same to mine, but I'm not answering. This behavior means they're on a manic swing. I told them to leave you alone."

"Like they would listen. I got several calls today. There's nothing to it? No new information I need to be aware of? I'd hate it if I didn't answer and they had a true emergency. Even stopped clocks are right twice a day, or whatever that old phrase is."

Rocky waved a finger in front of the camera. "Not that I can find. The usual money crap—they've run out of ways to be clever. Don't fall for it, Jess. They forced you to be their caretaker when you were just a child. Just because they're our parents doesn't turn them into good guys. They fucked with your head and are still doing it. If you allow it, they will take you down with them. As your sibling and someone who loves you, I'm telling you not to engage. I will handle them. I promise. Elaine is not in favor of any contact, but she will let me deal with them for your sake and our family. Vanessa is old enough to understand why my parents aren't around. She has no desire to be in their lives after everything that's happened. I've got a kid, Jess, and I have to protect her. But I also will protect my sister—as much as you will allow. I'd do more but respect your boundaries. Do not give in to their emotional blackmail. If you do, the demands will never stop. You have to be tempted. It's the guilt talking, the emotion they instilled in you."

She lowered her head and nodded. "Of course I am. What if we don't respond and this one time it's legit? How do I live with myself if I ignore them and that one time they had a true emergency?"

He blew out a long breath and touched the screen. "That stopped clock is wrong the rest of the time. The odds are not in their favor. I'll handle it. You've got me in your corner, sis. Do not answer the calls. Go for a jog or...do you have a boyfriend? If you do, get together with him. In any case, you need to visit soon."

"I do, and I promise I will when I can. The jury is out on the boyfriend situation." A million emotions tumbled through her mind so fast Jess wasn't sure which to tackle first. "I love you, Rocky."

His face reminded her of the few good times she'd had with her dad when he was sober. Those times, like his sobriety, had faded as she got older until memories were all she had. Those, and regrets.

"I love you back. I should have done more for you when you were eight. I cleared out and left you behind. It's my biggest regret. If I had it to do over again, I would have found a way to take you with me."

She pinched the bridge of her nose to quell the tears that threatened. Outside she picked out the noise of the band as they began to return from the club. Unlike the previous tour, they had no rooms to stay in and were going to get on the road for a wearying night of travel before their next destination.

"You did what you had to. If you hadn't left, they might have taken you down with them. We could have had a worse tragedy. You escaped and showed me that what I was going through wasn't forever. Besides, if I hadn't grown up that way, I wouldn't have all these great country songs to write." An idea started in the back of her mind, and she itched to reach for her guitar and notepad.

"Jess…"

"Thanks, Rocky. Your support means more than you can know. I will come visit soon, I promise."

He shifted his attention to the side, as though someone was just out of sight. "I hope so. Did I tell you that Vanessa is bugging me about learning the guitar? I don't need to tell you that the house is a lot less quiet than it used to be."

A memory of when she'd been trying to practice in her room before her mother came storming in telling her to "cut that racket" flowed through Jess. She must have been—she tried to recall. Twelve, maybe. Or thirteen.

"That's great. She takes after her aunt. I'm glad someone else besides me is bitten by the music bug. I'm here for her if she needs information. The band is coming into the bus. Thanks for the pep talk." The song started forming in her head, and Jess was itching to write it down before she forgot it.

"Promise me. Let me handle it."

"I will."

The hydraulic door whooshed open, and Benny and the rest piled on in a staggering heap that indicated they might have had a drink or two. It wasn't her concern.

"I'll call you when I've sorted out what's going on. Stay safe out there, little sis. I love you, and so does the family. You're important to us."

The words made warmth surge through her. If nothing else, she had this. "Love you back. Talk soon."

Jess hung up and reached for her guitar. The tune beating inside her had to come out. It flowed through her, a river that became a torrent. The melody that she'd started and Kai helped with took shape, the words flowing through her mind like a fast-moving river rushing downstream. Something took hold as though it had just been waiting for its opening. The last weeks noodling with the melody, and failing, now surged within her, showing her what she hadn't grasped until now.

Triumph flowed within her, despite the circumstances, despite the intrigue swirling around her. In the end, the thing she lived for, the music that satisfied her soul, had finally come to her.

Jess had a song to write.

Chapter Sixteen

When she got back from the tour, Jess asked to come over. Though he was aware he should say no, he didn't. Now she was here. As the bell rang, Kai made a final sweep of his living room. Everything was in order, as much as it could be. The bags of food were cooling on the table while the woman waited.

So many thoughts tumbled through him, and they all vanished when he took in the woman on his doorstep. He'd missed her these last few weeks but didn't have the words to express what went through his mind. Or rather, the ones that begged to be expressed stuck in his throat. He shouldn't let this continue, but she was so beautiful in a pair of jeans and a pink tank top that his heart ached. They had no future. There was no place in this universe for him and her. She deserved someone that made her life easier, not harder.

He wished it wasn't so right when she was in his arms.

"I'm glad you were free tonight. It's good to be home."

The words had so many connotations, so many suggestions. What he'd already arranged now lay heavy on his soul. He'd tossed a grenade into their night, and Jess didn't know it yet. He shouldn't have done it. "I hope the tour went well."

She made a seesaw motion with her hand. "About

the same. I did pick up some fans after the Ryder run, but that's about all. Gordon hasn't given us any indication when Shatter Sound will release a new song. Then again, he also hasn't let me go, so I suppose that's a victory. Michelle says hi. I dropped my stuff off and then came over."

The weeks apart hadn't altered his fundamental truth. Kai needed to solve his life before he tangled up with anyone else. He was aware what he'd done earlier was wrong, but she was here. What he'd set in motion couldn't be changed.

He already had the bags of Chinese food waiting, courtesy of one of the national chains. The reminder of what was inside them mocked him, and he wished he could take it back. "I hope you like what I got. You're American, but I think you will approve of my choices."

"Kai…" She frowned, her gaze going from the generic offerings and back to his face.

"This is good stuff." He'd done it as a challenge and, even as he was speaking, was aware he was being a jerk. He cleared his throat. Too late. He had to plow through, though he already wished he could change things. "The place is pretty Americanized, but it's tasty."

"Damn it."

He spooned some of the rice and chow mein onto his plate. "Eat," he said, setting the plate down on a mat and gesturing to the chopsticks.

Jess ignored his gesture. "No Singapore noodles? How about garlic-flavored beef? I don't mind chow mein and chop suey, but that's not my preference. You didn't even ask. Give me hot and sour soup and hot mint-leaves chicken any day of the week. I can't tell you what I like or don't like because you don't hear me. This is just one example of the larger issue. You think I'm too different from you, and nothing I do changes that. Even after all this time, you can fall back on that. You warned me at the beginning that you weren't in the place for a relationship, but I plowed right ahead despite that."

It would have been easier for Kai to agree. He could have said that she was superficial, and that would have done it. They would be over. "I wish that to be true, but it's not. It would have been so much simpler."

"Would it? Would you have gone to bed with me if I were that person you keep attempting to make me be? I get we're not destined for the long haul, but stop trying to make me fit your preconceived mold. It sucks, and I don't like it. I thought you were better than that. Why did you even invite me over if you're going to push me away? I was hoping this was going to be a fun evening, but you made it into a challenge. I just got back and was so excited to be with you, and now…this."

"You're right. In everything you say. I'm sorry."

Her body was still taut when he embraced her, and Kai cursed himself. He had blundered, hunting for an outlet for his hurt and confusion and landing it on the single human who didn't deserve it. The one who had always taken it.

He was an asshole.

****

Jess stayed stiff in his arms. His face had a hollowness to it, sorrow etched in the lines of his mouth and across his forehead.

"The one person who always backs me up and I turn on her. I was seeking somewhere to trauma dump, and I took it out on you. I am sorry, Jess. You didn't warrant being ambushed. You came here for a nice meal and company. I missed you, and I was wrong to behave the way I did. The excuses I can offer aren't worth the time it would take me to utter them. You have my sincerest apology for being a dick."

She bit her lip and refused to meet his eyes. "I was and you were. I didn't earn that kind of treatment. I've done nothing." She tried to hang on to the anger, but the pain written all over him made her resolve melt.

"No. You didn't. I've been taking my confusion out on you, and that is unworthy of me. And you. And us."

She held her breath, willing him to say more. When he didn't, she continued. "Thank you. I can't take it, Kai. Just because we're casual doesn't mean you should treat me as though I am disposable."

He cupped her face, and his dark eyes held more sorrow than she had anticipated. "You're right. I'll do better."

"I hope so." Her resolve wavered. She picked up her chopsticks so she could avoid his gaze. The heat of her anger still burned inside her, mixing with the joy of being with him again.

"I was an asshole, and I am sorry. You always make me feel like king of the world when you are the one who is special. People like you are rare."

Jess schooled her face into neutrality. She'd thought the words for a long time but never had the courage to say them. No time like the present, with the heat of her ire still burning inside her. She fought to find a way to express the words correctly and not like a challenge. "While we're on the subject, there's something I have to say."

The sight of her face reflected in his glasses made Jess falter. "You keep folks at a distance and don't let anyone in. You don't show that you're vulnerable. You aren't mainstream. You're a Buddhist, a vegetarian, you practice karate, and you used to run an avant-garde metal label. You're an outsider because you choose to be."

Kai didn't speak for long minutes, then met her gaze again. "You're right, though I'm not sure I admitted that to myself until this minute. I suppose that this chip I carry around on my shoulder is my own doing. I haven't been fair to you. I tried to believe you were shallow, because that would make it easier to fight my desire for you. I'm sorry. That was a terrible assumption, and you deserve better."

"Apology accepted." A beat of anger dwelled within her, but she pushed it aside. The important thing was that he was admitting his mistake. She closed her eyes and counted to ten. Old memories of dealing with tense situations flooded her. She couldn't deal with this anymore. People always liked to talk about themselves. She shouldn't have opened the door. "About Shatter Sound…what's your end date?"

If he was surprised by the abrupt shift, he didn't show it. Then again, Kai was as good at hiding his emotions as she was.

"Already gone. Gordon was glad to see the last of me." He gestured to the place where their food still sat, cooling. "We should eat before this gets colder."

"He's stupid to release you, but neither one of us have any say in that. If I'm on the chopping block, there's nothing I can do. Since you're at loose ends, do you think you could help me? I have to figure out my next move, if and when Shatter Sound drops me. Yes, I have a manager, but I could use someone who's been around the business and has familiarity with how it works. If not, it's fine. You have the right to say no."

"It could be anytime now." He met her gaze.

She stared back at him without flinching. "I can't stop what is going to happen. I think he regretted signing me as soon as he did so. Country was new to him, and he saw dollar signs. He believed he would ride a wave of a California country-artist revolution. When I didn't have instant success, he lost interest. I've been doing all I can to make it work, but I'm not dumb."

"If it does happen, I'm partly responsible. That's why Gordon brought me on. Yet even with that, you'd still want to work with me?"

She considered all the ways to answer the question. "That's business. Thank you for trying. Now, will you help me?"

"I'd love to. I've got nothing but time. Thanks for thinking of me."

Before she could say something she regretted, she gestured at the table. "Thank you. Can we call a different place and order better dishes?"

His grin would have rivaled the sun. "By all means."

****

Mingled scents of spices and turpentine wafted through the living room of Terri and Clarke's condo when Terri opened the door. Kai smiled and hugged the woman who had been instrumental in trying to keep his label afloat.

Terri motioned to the end of the hallway. "Clarke's in his studio chasing his muse. I'm making some curry. It should be ready soon if you can to stay for lunch."

That neither of them had succeeded was not due to the long hours and sweat she put into the effort. Terri August threw herself into everything she did, whether that be work, life, or love.

"I expected to find you nose deep in soufflés or something similar since you're learning new dishes in that fancy culinary school you're going to." Kai smiled at his former vice president.

She gave him a grin and ushered him into the kitchen. "That hasn't started yet, but Clarke is awaiting the fruits of my soon-to-be labors. In the meantime, I'm trying some Thai recipes. Care to taste? Are you hungry?"

He followed her to where a skillet was bubbling. The scent of curry and coconut milk blended together. His stomach rumbled.

She stopped. "Shoot, you're a vegetarian. Can you eat around the chicken, or is that not allowed?"

He raised a hand. "I dropped in without warning. You don't need to feed me."

"I can make something else. Oh, I haven't put the chicken in yet. I'll separate the pans and create one with tofu." She began fussing around the kitchen, searching the cupboards. Her movements reminded him of all the times they worked late into the night on projects—all in vain. A pang of sadness for his label went through him.

Accept the things you cannot change… "Thank you for feeding a hungry intruder."

She gave him a fast grin that reminded him of the man who had become her husband. Kai didn't have the entire backstory behind Clarke and Terri, but had been told enough. She had been obsessed with Clarke ten years earlier, and Clarke rejected her. From what Kai had learned, that hurt lingered into the current times until they worked through it. The duo was solid now, deeply in love, and those first days put aside, if not forgotten.

Clarke entered the room and greeted Kai with a wave and a "hey, man." The smell of his labors followed him.

Terri pushed at her husband. "From the amount of paint on you, I'd say you're making headway on your latest project. Will you do an unveiling anytime soon?"

He gave her a wide smile that had been part of Clarke's rock-star persona back when the band made the top ten on the charts. Now that grin had substance behind it and not the temporary flash of a huckster.

Clarke Masters was a better man after falling in love.

"Not yet. When the time comes, I'll trade you for some fancy cooking." Clarke met Kai's gaze. "I'd shake your hand, but you'd be multicolored afterward. Great to have you here—it's been too long. Terri told me about Shatter Sound. Can't say I'm sorry."

"In the end, I'm not either, though my bank account may disagree."

She stirred the contents of the skillet and then turned off the heat. "They gave Ally the promotion because they had to. If he didn't, Gordon would lose her and Dirk. The label might survive the loss of one, but not both." Terri stumbled and waved her hand at him. "Forget you heard that, Kai. That's not public."

Kai inclined his head. "I assumed something happened when Dirk no longer came to meetings. The story is he's working from home. Don't worry, old friend. I won't tell tales."

Terri gave him a fast smile. "You never do. So yeah, they had a blowout. Gordon tried to push Ally out when he discovered the two were an item, and Dirk told him to fuck off—in his own style—and quit on the spot. He's gone. Not sure where. He fell off the radar."

"Though we are very different, Dirk is a good man. I applaud him for doing what was right."

Kai kept his own counsel about the conversations he'd had with Dirk. If nothing came of it, nobody would be disappointed. Terri had always been his rock, but she had her own concerns now. He had to find his own way. The news that Ally and Dirk had been dating wasn't a surprise either. Love was all around him.

For him too if he accepted it.

Clarke leaned over and pressed a kiss to Terri's lips. "Never met the guy, but if he's good for one of Terri's friends, that's enough for me. What brings you here, Kai?"

Before Kai could answer, Terri focused on the pot. "Try this before I separate the pans, and tell me what you think. My love here adores all my dishes, so I could use an unbiased opinion."

Terri's quick glance at Clarke stilled whatever the former singer had been about to say, judging by the way he opened his mouth and then shut it.

Kai accepted the spoon she handed him. The mingled spices exploded on his taste buds, and he sighed in appreciation. "I suppose I shouldn't be surprised you went this route. You always did bring in amazing food. You're fantastic with organization and numbers, but you're a great cook too. This is delicious."

Her triumphant beam was accompanied by a bark of laughter from Clarke.

"I told you. It's not just me, my love. I'll shower, and we'll eat. Stay for lunch, Kai. We haven't gotten to catch up in too long."

Terri bustled around the kitchen while Kai watched.

After a few minutes, she moved the skillet off the heat.

"That needs to sit for the full flavor to emerge." She focused on Kai. "We've been friends for several years. Once upon a time you gave me some sage advice, and I've never regretted taking it. Will you tell me what's going on, or do I have to drag it out of you?"

He raked his hand through his hair, wishing he'd worn his glasses. Jess' words about them putting a barrier between him and those around him echoed. "I've been at loose ends since Apposite collapsed. Going on tour with Jessica meant more than missing your wedding."

"We don't care about that—" Terri began, but Kai continued, riding over her.

"I took the consultancy at Shatter Sound because I didn't have anything else to do. Maybe I shouldn't have. I was there to do the dirty work Gordon wouldn't. That it didn't pan out the way he anticipated doesn't change that fact. I find it difficult to be in a subordinate role. But it also introduced me to someone. Jessica."

"You always did the tough stuff at the label. I suppose Gordon presumed you would continue that. Asshole. And by Jessica you mean the singer? The one you were helping?"

He laughed with no mirth. "Yes."

"Oh. Wow. You got with her? Is it serious?"

"For her."

Terri shook her head. "Don't be a jerk. That's not like you. At least, I hope it isn't."

He lowered his head, letting his hair cover his face so she couldn't detect his emotions. "You're right, as always. It's not simple. Jessica is…rare. Special. She's an old soul in a young body, but the fact is that she is still ten years younger than me. I had no business getting involved in the first place. I am not casual about sex."

From somewhere down the hall, a voice broke out. Clarke was singing a tune that Kai identified as one of Attraction's, his former band's, biggest hits.

Amusement danced over Terri's face even as she made an exasperated sound. "No, you aren't. I'm happy for you. It's time you found a girlfriend."

Kai focused on the bubbling food on the stove. "She's too young for me."

"That's crap."

He snorted at the indelicate word. His ex-vice president had learned a thing or two from her husband. "It's the truth."

"Nah. Age is a state of mind. If you're scared, just say so. I won't judge. We've been through a lot, and you were there when my life was falling apart. It's okay, but don't stay in that fear. That gets you nowhere."

The singing broke off, and the shower stopped.

Kai stared at his former vice president and then made a low sound of pain. "I have no idea what to do."

****

The ever-present blare of the television greeted her when Jess entered the room. Michelle was hunched over her computer, either chatting or placing bets. Michelle's life was none of Jess' concern.

"Anything interesting happening?" she asked, gesturing to the machine.

"Yeah. Lots. Your ex Craig came by. He said for you to call him when you're back."

Jess' brow furrowed at the message from Craig. That wasn't like him. They had stayed friends after their affair was over, but it had been a year since they broke up. Over time, as with most things, their contact had become more distant. Still, his behavior in Bakersfield had been out of character too. Maybe this was just more of the same.

Jess picked up her cell to return his calls, but before she could dial, it rang. The incoming number verified that Craig was calling. Again.

At least it wasn't her parents, but she was sure they'd be hounding her again soon. Just because they'd gone quiet meant little.

"Hey, Craig," she said, unease crawling through her. She didn't like this sudden change. Too many things had happened in the recent past. "Where's the fire?"

He chuckled, but it sounded a little forced. "I was listening to a country song on the radio, and it made me think of you. I decided to stop by to say hi and catch up."

"Thanks." She twined her hand around a lock of hair and toyed with it, waiting for him to come to the point.

"Can I come over? I have something to say."

She fought to control the urge to say no. She would have preferred to be alone, but he had something on his mind, and she was used to putting her needs aside. She couldn't bear to have one more person blowing up her phone. This was Craig, not some stranger.

"Sure. Come on by."

When he arrived, Jess pushed the door open to admit him. Once upon a time she might have been okay giving him a hug and a kiss, but his taut frame suggested she should keep her distance. The unease that had started when he called prompted her to shift away. Michelle waved at him and then exited into her bedroom, shutting the door behind her.

"What's going on? Michelle said you kept calling."

Jess motioned to the living room, not saying how that persistence made her react. She chose the standalone chair as opposed to the sofa. Craig stood, frowning, making her wonder if he'd hoped they would sit together.

"I tried to reach you. To talk to you." He gazed out the window and to the hills that separated Hollywood from the San Fernando Valley.

"I was out, but I'm back now. I would have answered your text when I got home."

"Tell me about this Kai Halara guy."

She stiffened. "What about him?"

He started to pace, his footsteps loud in the room. He shoved his hands in his pockets and came back to stand in front of her. His position made her fight not to jump up and put distance between them. She was being ridiculous. This was Craig, and they had been friends before their romance and after.

"How serious are you?"

"That's not a question I can answer." Jess fought not to show her reluctance to discuss this with Craig. "We take it day by day, without putting labels on it."

To her relief, he didn't touch her. A sound escaped his lips, and he rocked back when she refused to meet his gaze.

"You love him." The words were strangled, the syllables harsh. "Like all the way—for real?"

She struggled to explain the situation to the man she had tried to love. A man worth loving. He was a good man.

But he wasn't Kai.

"Yes."

"Does he love you?"

She pushed out of the chair to get the distance she

169

craved. She didn't want to have this conversation. Not with Craig.

Not with anyone not named Kai.

"As I said, we don't put labels on it."

"Jessie," he cried. "That's not good enough. You should have love."

"That's for me to figure out. Kai has shown me something remarkable. It will have to be enough."

He crossed the room and fell to his knees, grasping her hands in his. "It shouldn't be. You inspire love. But you do it so under the radar we don't appreciate it until you are gone. I'm here to beg you to give us a second chance."

She blinked, contemplating how to slide away from him. Nothing she could do would seem any less than what she intended. A refusal. "What?"

"We could try again. Kai doesn't love you. We loved each other once. We can do so again. Please. Let's start over. For what we were and could be. I'll find a way to handle your folks this time. I'll do better."

This couldn't be happening.

You left me alone when I needed you.

"You dumped me because my family was horrible. You said that you couldn't deal with them. That was your choice, and I accepted it. It's too late. We can't go back."

"I was wrong. Jess, we were good together. When I figured out what was going on with that man, I realized what a terrible mistake I made. You haven't dated anyone else until Kai. I had it in the back of my mind that maybe when I was ready, you'd come back. That was arrogant. I'm sorry. I shouldn't have tried to keep you on a shelf. But this guy, he doesn't love you."

She pushed away from him, doing what she'd

yearned to do all along. To her relief, he accepted the distance.

"As I said, it's too late. We can't focus on the past." Her voice was shaking as her insides trembled. She wished she was far away from this. She forced herself to speak. "It's over. I can't give you what you're asking for. I'm sorry. I'd like to stay friends, but that's all."

Craig's lips tightened, and she prayed he wasn't about to continue to protest.

"If you guys broke up…"

She shook her head. He wavered in place as he glanced at the door.

"Even if we did, you and I have sailed. I hate to be so blunt, Craig, but we can't have any misunderstanding. This has to be one and done." Her therapist's voice echoed in her mind, lending her strength. *You have emotional rights too, Jessica.* "You left me. Remember? Not that I didn't understand, but I could have used the support. I got over it because I had to, just like everything else." *Just like everyone else.*

"You said you understood. That you'd do the same. We stayed friends. I guess I always assumed that you accepted it."

His confusion had her wishing she'd been blunt back then. She was going to need to talk to her therapist some more. Baby steps.

She searched her mind for the right way to express herself without damaging his feelings.

There wasn't any.

"I did, but I also didn't. The truth is that I hoped you'd stay and deal with the insanity. I acknowledged that the situation was too much for you, but that didn't mean your rejection didn't hurt. I'm not made of stone."

Her heart sank at the stricken gasp he let out at her words. Harsh truths were better kept to themselves where they couldn't hurt people.

"That's not fair."

"Life isn't fair. I learned that a long time ago." The words slipped out despite her notion that she wouldn't do any more damage.

His breath whooshed out. "Damn, Jessie."

She would not take it back. She could not take it back. She stood there, not speaking all the reassuring words that rushed up inside her. The sentiments wouldn't be true. She'd be lying to him—and to herself.

He ducked his head. "Even if you guys broke up, then that doesn't mean that you and me have a chance? We're done for good?"

She shook her head, and his shoulders sagged.

"Kai and I have nothing to do with you and me. When we end, I will figure out the next steps, but that's on me."

To his credit, Craig did nothing more than shift from one foot to the other, his face falling. "That's what I came here to find out." He met her gaze, and she tried not to flinch. She owed him that much.

"I'd like to still be friends." She started to say more, but nothing came to mind.

"I wish things had been different. I'm going to need some time. I'll call you when I'm ready. I don't want to lose you from my life, but I can't do this right now."

"Do what you have to. I'm not used to being so blunt, but I'm trying to change." She wondered if they would ever be the same. Perhaps she and Craig could have continued the way they were, but he'd forced it. Now she couldn't escape the consequences—and found she didn't mind.

He gave her a brisk nod. "Though it hurts, I do appreciate the honesty. Better to have it all out in the open. You were always so slippery before. That's part of what made me think you'd be waiting when I was ready to come back. My mistake. I…yeah, I should go. Thanks for the blast of honesty."

Jess understood she could still call him back, stop him, say the words Craig almost begged her to utter. She could have what she'd sought from him when they first got together. A solid man with a good path forward. One who had a stable future and a good head on his shoulders. One who never confused her.

One who never touched her heart.

"You're welcome. I'm sorry it's not what you hoped to hear. It's not an easy truth, but it's mine."

To her surprise, he stopped and came back to her. He placed a hand on her shoulder. "I hate that it's that way, but, Jess, do yourself a favor and be honest. It hurts you less in the long run."

"Craig…"

"I'll be fine. I should have been stronger back then, but it's too late now. Take care. I'll be in touch when I'm ready."

She let him go and didn't try to stop him.

Chapter Seventeen

The next day, Jess was at Kai's house, in his living room, when the song rushed through her, and she forgot about her name and where she was. She let go of anything but needing a guitar and laying the song down before she lost the thread. "Kai, I need your help. Can I borrow a guitar and sheet music, if you have it?"

Kai nodded to the back of the room. "Guitar, yes. Sheet music, no." He went to a closet where he took out a guitar that must have been a promotional item, judging by the branding. He crossed the room and handed it to her. "It needs tuning."

He started to say more, but she snatched the instrument from his hands.

"I wish you had something for me to put the notes on. I need to get this down." She tested the strings and tuned the guitar until she was satisfied. Then she began strumming the melody that beat like a trapped bird in her chest.

"I'll record you. You can transcribe it later."

"Sure. Go ahead."

She wasted no more time releasing the tune that flowed out of her, waiting to burst forth. The song was one of sadness, of sorrow, that touched all the pain that lay inside her from all the years of neglect and abuse from the parents who were supposed to protect her. It wasn't of blame, but of survival. Her entire life mingled together to erupt into a clean, haunting tune that made her shiver all the way to her toes.

She stumbled, the words faltering as emotion caught up with her. Jess paused and took a deep breath. She was aware that Kai was still recording her on his phone, but that didn't matter. This had to be set free. The sole sounds in the house were the refrigerator in the kitchen nearby and Jess playing her new song. The one she'd been working on for a lifetime, though she hadn't been cognizant of that until this instant.

When she was satisfied, she lifted her fingers from the guitar and bent her head, her hair falling over her face. The rush of the last month came over her then, from the relationship with Kai, to the uncertainty at the label, to Craig, to the harassment by her parents. She didn't move or give any outward show, but the tears came, trickling down her cheeks without any accompanying sound.

She wasn't aware that Kai had stopped recording until he eased the guitar from her neck. She let it slide to the floor, too spent by what she had just put down to do anything else. Then he was folding her in his arms, and she went into his embrace, all her pent-up emotions racking her shaking body. She allowed herself to release everything except right now. The world shifted as she breathed in his presence. He moved his palms up and down her back in a rhythmic motion until the pain started to ease from her soul.

She lifted her head from his shoulder, and he met her gaze. The smoky passion on his face made her breath catch. She was a realist and could expect no more than desire from him. Right now, though, none of that mattered.

"That was remarkable. You are extraordinary. Such depth. Jessica, you are a wonder."

"Thanks." She dabbed at his shirt, damp with her tears. "I feel…lighter."

"As you should." He smoothed her hair back from her cheek and pressed a kiss to her lips. "That song is brilliant, and so are you." He moved to kiss her again when his phone rang.

The sound was shrill and loud in the room, and Jess started. The poetry was gone. "You still have a landline?"

Jess allowed herself a minute to hope that he was in this deeper than just lust. But she had to let go of expectations. She was too old and too smart to allow foolish hopes get in her way. She'd just poured that into a song that was damned good. She'd have to be happy with that.

He still didn't move. "My parents are terrified of earthquakes, and Mom has trotted out a million statistics about how it's easier to get a call out on a landline than a cell phone in the event of the Big One."

Jess' laugh was shaky.

"It's never anyone I need to talk to, unless I wish to purchase solar panels. Or drought-tolerant landscaping. Both of which I already have."

The knot inside her started to ease. Everything was going to be okay. Whatever happened, she was a survivor.

The line clicked over to the machine. To her surprise, the voice on the line belonged to Ally.

"Kai? Are you there?"

He levered off the floor and went to the phone. "I'm here. This is unexpected."

Jess picked up the guitar and placed it on the black sofa as her puzzled gaze went to Kai.

He was standing in his workout sweats and nothing else, his body language shifting until tension radiated from him. "Oh. That changes things. Yes, she's here." He motioned her over with a quick flip of his hand.

She went, though her fight-or-flight instinct was telling her to run.

He held the handset out to her. "Ally asked to talk to you."

Anxiety curled around her spine as the desire to flee intensified. All she wished to do was back away from the phone and sprint for the exit.

Instead, she took it from Kai with almost nerveless fingers and wiped at her still damp face. He stood next to her but didn't touch her. His breath shuddered, and a tremor rippled through him.

"Ally? Why are you calling me on Kai's landline? I didn't even know he had one until just now." Dread crawled over her skin. Ally Wilson was a practical woman. If she was hunting Jess down, something was wrong.

Jess had a bad feeling about what was to come. She wished Ally wasn't still speaking. Blood roared through her body, making thinking difficult.

"Sorry to interrupt, but this couldn't wait."

Jess already anticipated what Ally's next words would be. "What's going on? Why did you have to find me right away? I'm not missing any promo, am I? I have reminders set for those, just in case."

Ally didn't speak for a second, and when she did, her voice was toneless and flat. "I just got word that Shatter Sound dropped you. You must not be checking your cell. I didn't want you to hear it from anyone else."

Kai moved and retrieved her phone from where she kept it in her handbag. She had the ringer off, and sure enough, she had three missed calls. Two were from her manager, and one was from Gordon.

"Thanks, Ally. Do you have any idea when it takes effect? How much time do I have to close things out?"

Ally sucked in a breath. "I understand it's immediate. I'm sorry."

The anxiety that had been moving through her body exploded into reality. The primitive part of her longed to curl up and press her head to her knees. She'd tried so hard and failed. This was ashes around her, like the rest of her life. It wasn't fair. "Thank you. I'd better call my manager. I appreciate you going the extra mile to find me."

"Of course. If there's anything I can do, say the word."

Jess wouldn't, but she didn't need to tell Ally that. Her dream was over, lying in shattered bits at the bottom of a corporate spreadsheet.

She had no idea what she was going to do now. She held out her arms. "Kai, will you make love to me?"

He drew her to him but shook his head as he was doing so. "Perhaps that isn't for the best. We should talk."

She fought for words to express to him the depth of her emotions. "No. I can't think right now. Make love to me. Please."

For a horrible heartbeat, she thought he was going to say no. She couldn't bear to be said no to one more time.

Then he rolled her T-shirt up and freed her breasts

from the cups of her bra. "I will do whatever is right for you."

They touched just with their lips as he held her in his arms, and her torso pressed to his.

"This. This is right. This is everything."

His indrawn breath seared her senses.

"My bedroom," he whispered.

She gave him her lips, and again without preamble he delved between her lips and into her waiting mouth. His tongue tangled with hers, tasting, dueling, thrusting again and again as he moved. She slid her hands under his armpits and over the muscled breadth of his shoulders, digging her nails into his skin for traction.

"Jess," he called on a choked sob, raining kisses over her face.

She had intended to do the touching, to feel his powerful body, but his caresses were too good to stop, and she surrendered to his touch.

With her help he stripped her shirt and bra off her and dumped them to the ground without ceremony. Then his tongue and lips were tasting her breasts as he loved to do, licking, then sucking, then biting while he suckled.

A throaty moan escaped Jess, and she buried her fingers in his silky black hair, memorizing the tingling her palms got whenever she touched his shining locks. She willed herself not to let her emotions show. Nothing could break the spell. "You've got on too many clothes."

"You too." His voice was raspy.

By tacit approval each tended to their own clothing, stripping it off as fast as they could before turning to each other.

She reached down and circled his base, stroking the length of him.

He encouraged her strokes by placing his hand over hers, reminding her of the pattern he liked. His breath shortened, his chest rising and falling.

He let out a fierce exhalation. "No more. Not right now," he pleaded. "Not like this."

She released him, and he bored her back down to the bed, his mouth once again fastened on hers.

He rained kisses over her collarbone and shoulders and down past her breasts to her waist. Kai ran a line of pleasure down one side and then the other before delving his tongue into her navel.

Jess jerked and tried to move him up.

He paused and gazed up at her from under a curtain of hair. "You never let me finish, and I'm always too hot for you to resist burying myself inside you. I want to taste you, to love you that way. Please."

It would be a treasured memory, one to last a lifetime. She nodded, and his face lit up with primal male satisfaction.

Jessica spread her legs wider, and Kai settled himself between them. His elbows pressed open her inner thighs, widening her farther to him.

She moaned again, throwing her head back to the soft pillows piled at the head of his bed.

He blew a current of air into her and licked up and down, up and down, taking his time as Jess started to shake. She tried to imprint his tongue inside her on her memory banks, but all she could do was gasp as he caressed her. Her fingers settled on his shoulders as he circled her clit, which was hard and begging for his touch.

"Oh…" she whispered.

He tilted his head up, his mouth shiny and his hair

falling across his face in dark strands. "This time I will love you all the way."

She fell back, and he bent to her again. His strands tickled her inner thighs, a caress that further inflamed her.

Soon Jess was moaning, clutching at the comforter as he took her. Her hips moved in counterpoint to his strokes until he gripped her in his teeth in a sensual threat.

She shrieked at the bite and thrust in one quick, savage motion. He used his elbows to hold her down again and began suckling her hard, drawing her flesh into his mouth and lashing over it.

She shuddered, the universe passing before her vision as her body tensed and then flew apart in the most intense orgasm she'd ever experienced, streamers of ecstasy emptying from every pore as she screamed. The pleasure went on and on, until the shuddering slowed and Jess' death grip on the comforter loosened.

"Kiss me," she said when she could speak.

"I taste like you," he protested.

She tugged him up, and thankfully, he didn't resist. She pressed a kiss to his lips and did taste herself and mint and the faint aftertaste of garlic.

He wrapped his arm around her neck for a hard embrace before settling her back on the bed again. "Now then." He reached into the nightstand and produced a condom. She recognized it as their favorite brand.

He rolled it onto himself with shaking fingers and then urged her legs open. She parted them, still wet from his lovemaking.

"You have the most superb body. I'll never forget." She moved her hips and took a little bit more of him. She yearned to be filled by him, experience the exquisite pleasure of having this man inside her.

Kai sank all the way to the hilt. "Oh God, you always fit me so tight, so perfect." He thrust, pulling out and then sinking in again. Each time he was a little slicker, a little harder, until he moaned and stopped.

He gathered her to him. Jess clung to him, to the broad muscles of his back. His heart was pounding so loud the sound was all that echoed in her ears.

"Jess, I…" He threw back his head, his teeth bared. Pushing her back down to the comforter again, he began thrusting, his arms shaking as he held himself above her. Then he was crying out inarticulate sounds as he poured his essence into her, his orgasm like that of a summer thunderstorm, wild, savage, and elemental.

The wild abandon of the tableau gripped her, and before Jess realized what she was saying, she shouted, "I love you."

Then he was surrounding her, enveloping her with his presence. He wrapped around her, enfolding her in his skin, his scent, his warmth.

She'd lost everything, but she had this.

For now.

Chapter Eighteen

Kai handed the papers back to Jess, wishing he could take the pain away from her defeated posture. She kept shuffling the pages dropping her from Shatter Sound Records as though they were one of those three-card-monte frauds con men played.

This was no trick.

Her manager and lawyer had negotiated the details, but Kai insisted he review it before she sign anything. Now, less than a week later, she had the contract severing her relationship with Shatter Sound.

"Your advance is yours to keep. Any reputable label would do the same. I recommended that you attempt to get a reversion of copyright clause to gain back your masters. Right now, they own everything, but they may be willing to let you buy the rights back for a set amount. Do you have it if they do?"

She shook her head. "No. The amount was pretty paltry, and I stuck it in a CD rather than spend it. I don't have extra money to get the rights back. In essence, they have my stuff and I'm screwed?"

He put his hand on her back and stroked her. He wished he had magic words to say something to take the pain away, but didn't. "To what is on the record, yes. That's theirs unless we can come to some different arrangement. I've gotten them to strike the clause regarding any rights they have over your forthcoming

183

works. They didn't fight very hard—better to give in on this common point than drag this out. That reluctance works to your advantage. With your future songs being your own, you can take any of the unrecorded stuff to a different label. You will have to have the ability to have unfettered access to those to move forward."

Her face was etched in lines of misery. "All right. Thanks."

He knelt in front of her. "It's a setback, but it's not the end. Dreams fail. We get new ones."

She nodded but lifted her gaze from his, focusing on the wall beyond and saying nothing.

"Jessica. I understand. You can take this as a loss and let it define you, or you can use it to determine what happens next."

She got to her feet, emotion blazing in her eyes. "That's what you did, isn't it, Kai? You just rebounded and went on with your life after your label went under. Is that what you've been doing? Because it sure feels like you've been wallowing in your own version of failure and shutting out the world."

"It's not the same." He drew back, putting several steps between himself and the woman.

She heaved out a breath, the sound loud in the room. "Isn't it? How is it not? You said you lost your dream— so did I. Signing the contract was the greatest day of my life. Now it's all in shambles because I couldn't make it work. How is it different? Your label failed, and more than me were affected, so maybe it's me on a macro scale, but I think the two are a lot alike. Don't you dare dismiss my emotions just because you think yours are more valid. I didn't take you for that kind of man."

He was dying to stay mad. But the sight of her tragic

composure under the rage cooled his fire. The pages releasing her from Shatter Sound stared at him, accusatory and stark. He'd signed something similar when he sold his catalog, and the devastation still haunted him. "Point taken. I was minimizing what you're going through when I had no right to."

She whooshed out a breath. "I…thank you."

He went back to her and tugged on her arms until she relented. To his dismay, she was trembling, though she tried to conceal it.

"How can I help?" He gestured in the direction of the papers. "I have connections…" He let it trail off, but his meaning was clear.

"No. Forget it." She straightened her shoulders, throwing off whatever idea he'd planted. "I am not using our friendship to advance my career."

A frisson of displeasure shot through him. "I offered."

"I said no. I failed. What if I take you down too? You don't need to lift up a failed musician when you've got problems of your own."

Kai rocked her, touched beyond words at this supreme show of her vulnerability. "That is of little importance. This is something I want to do."

She was shaking her head as he spoke, and he understood that she would refuse.

It troubled him more than he would admit. He had been imagining all sorts of things that he should not. Jessica Baker was at a crossroads. Freeing her from the restrictions of the label was a gift that she couldn't see yet, but she would, in time. Shatter Sound had given her back her future. She no longer had anyone to report to or any restrictions to be bound by. She was her own agent, with endless possibilities ahead of her.

That was why he had to let her go. She'd been released from her label and was at loose ends. She could move to Nashville to make a fresh start, or Austin, somewhere that wasn't Los Angeles. He would be doing her a kindness if he ended things. Then she'd have nothing tying her here. She could change cities and try and make it work again. She was a country artist. She should be in Nashville. She loved him, and that emotion was holding her back. Kai needed to let her go.

That was what he had to do. He couldn't imagine how he was going to manage it.

****

"Kai?"

After repeated knocking had yielded no answer, Jess tried Kai's front door. Finding it unlocked, she pushed the door open, calling his name as she did so.

"Kai?" she called again, wondering at the complete stillness of the house. She couldn't detect any motion. Not even the breeze was willing to disturb the quiet of the house.

"In here." His words were coming from his den.

She breathed a sigh of relief. For a minute she had wondered if he was hurt...or worse. She couldn't imagine him doing anything drastic but wasn't sure where her fantasy ended and he began. She had to live in this reality and not the one she'd dared to dream in the middle of the night. He was hurting, and that was what she had to focus on. Though foreboding washed over her, she forced herself to move forward.

The den was done in muted browns and russets, soothing earth tones that matched the tranquility of the room. It faced the backyard with its high walls and leafy trees. A mat was set up on the floor, and there wasn't much furniture.

He was sitting cross-legged, his face impassive.

Jess sat down next to him and slid a hand up his thigh. Kai's gaze darkened to that coal black he got when he was experiencing something he found difficult to put a name to.

She moved her hand over his chest, memorizing the contours. She'd been expecting this, like a condemned woman expecting the executioner's axe. Though every inch of her yearned to turn and go, she stayed. She had to do this.

Sometimes the executioner was a blessing. At least then the waiting was over.

"This relationship isn't fair to you."

She snorted. "Life isn't fair. I learned that a long time ago." She cast her mind back to Craig and the way he'd tried to get her to go back to him. But the two situations were different—or perhaps that was wishful thinking. In the end, perhaps all romances had tragic endings. "I said to myself when this time came that I would accept it and go. I will. I know when to fold my cards and all that."

She could tell by his puzzled air that Kai didn't get the reference. They were from separate worlds and in different places in their lives. This should be a relief. Now she would have nobody to deal with but herself.

"I'm doing what is best for both of us."

Jess' scoffing was loud in the quiet room. She got to her feet, the urge to run replaced by a slow simmering rage that started at the bottom of her stomach and radiated outward. "Please don't give me some speech about how it's not me, it's you. I've gotten that more than once, and in the recent past, though Shatter Sound may not be the right analogy. It's a lot of BS."

"Terri said something similar." He stood, and they stared at each other.

The anger suffused her, making Jess tremble. "Terri?"

"My friend. Ally's friend. She's now married to Clarke Masters."

"You guys talked about me?" The urge to flee was so strong that she had to clasp her hands together to keep her rooted to her spot.

"We did. She said…that doesn't matter now. Jessica, I will always remember you. This. Us. But it's better for both of us that we end this now. Before someone gets hurt."

Her peal of laughter—more pain than mirth—shattered the afternoon. "I told you how I feel. Don't you think it's too late?"

He bowed his head. "As always, your wisdom is greater than mine. For what it's worth, I'm sorry."

Not enough to change your mind, though. "Well. I learned long ago that sorry doesn't get it done. You do what you have to, Kai, but don't pretty it up for my benefit."

He padded into the living room barefoot, and Jess followed.

"All right. I won't. You've been aware all along that I was in transition in my life and couldn't offer you forever. You accepted it." He paused.

She couldn't help but hope that he wasn't going to do this. That for once in her life she, Jessica Baker, was enough. But she never had been. Not for her parents, not for her boyfriends, not for Shatter Sound or her fans, and one hundred percent not for Kai Halara, the man who'd been eluding her this entire time. She'd had him in body but never in spirit.

She had always understood this would be the outcome. She just didn't expect it to burn like fire.

Jess squared her shoulders and tried to keep her face impassive. She'd had a lifetime of pain to learn how to cope, but this one went deeper than anything she'd ever experienced. Still, she was a survivor. She could do this.

She had in the past and would again. That's who she was.

"I did, and I won't bother saying that you've been confusing over the last weeks, because at the end of the day, whatever you said, despite the passion you showed me, you can always come back to the fact you warned me at the beginning you couldn't give me forever. I'd been a fool to expect anything more. So don't spare me now. Lay it all on me." She would not cry. Not after everything. She had to be strong one final time. She was Jessica Baker, and she'd been through worse. She could do this.

Kai's shoulders slumped. That gave her a measure of satisfaction, cruel though that might have been.

"Fair enough. I did say that at the start. Jess, there's more. I'm up for a job as the president of Plausive Records. My career might be restarted soon."

"Oh, is that right?" The emotion that surged through her surprised her with its intensity, bitter words that fought to be spoken flooding her mouth with bile. She couldn't speak at that moment, because those furious syllables could never be taken back. All the past hurts danced inside her like individual fireflies, their every sting its own bright light.

Jess glared at him, clenching her teeth against the fury she wasn't screaming out loud.

****

He'd made a mistake. He couldn't be sure why he'd said it. He was letting her go, and he didn't need to dump salt on the wound. Yet he had.

Maybe he'd had it right before. He was an asshole.

"A new job and now you're dumping me? Convenient timing."

He slanted his gaze to her fierce beauty shimmering in the sunlight in his living room. The light put the lower part of her face into shadow. He wished he couldn't make out her eyes. The wounded pain, the hurt in them of things unsaid, pierced him to the core.

Kai ran his hand over his hair. "I suppose I understand why you would believe that. I am not sure if I'm going to accept Plausive if they offer, or strike out on my own. It's that uncertainty that makes this impossible. Until I have a better sense of what I do next, the timing isn't there. Until I'm established again, I'm no good for anyone. You have your whole life ahead of you, and I have no right to take you down with me."

"Little unsuccessful country singer isn't good enough for a big bad executive, is that it, Kai? Or do you think I would expect you to sign me if we were still fucking?" Bitterness edged her voice, and she pushed to the far side of the room.

He searched for words to make it better but had nothing. "If anything, it's the reverse. I botched this once, and there's no guarantee it won't happen again. That's why this has to be done. I can't give you what you deserve."

Jess closed her eyes. He thought he'd be grateful to

be away from their deep shadows, but her tense body was its own condemnation.

"We both failed, so that's a lot of crap. Leave me with the dignity of recognizing my own mind." A myriad of emotions flew over her face, and she heaved out a long sigh.

"We are in different stages of our lives. None of this is fair to you."

"Didn't you say it wasn't the age of the person but the age of the soul? Ten years can't matter."

"Even so." Kai focused on the katana on the wall, but the ceremonial weapon was the furthest thing from his consciousness.

She drew in a harsh breath. "My begging days are over."

He flinched at the words and forced himself to focus on her again. He should say something…had to make it clear. He opened his mouth, and she held up her hand.

"Just…don't. I'm not going to apologize for loving you, though, even if it's something you didn't ask for. I'm not going to make a scene or anything. I'll go, like I told myself I would when this first started. Even if it's like I made a deal with the devil." She laughed, the sound harsh. "Oh yeah, that's a concept you don't believe in."

"I'm not sure anymore."

Jess went to where she'd dropped her purse and picked it up. He stayed motionless, his body swaying in place. He couldn't do this. He had to do this.

"Fuck you, Kai Halara. All of this is bullshit. Window dressing. Be man enough to say that you had your fun and now it's over. Don't dress it up in some holier-than-thou crapola, because I'm not buying it. You say we're done, fine. I'm not going to argue. I wouldn't stay with you now if you begged me. You've made it very clear I come nowhere on your list of priorities, and that's not who I will spend my life with. I got plenty of that growing up. At least my parents were honest about what they required from me. Booze and a soft room to drink it in. You pretty it up in fancy syllables, but the outcome is the same. Our time is up. When I walk out that door, you won't ever be with me again. It's over."

He fought not to beg her to stay. But if he let it go on any longer, he would speak different words, and he couldn't do that. Jess needed to be free to reach for her next goal and wouldn't do that with him in the picture. She had to focus on her career and not him. He was letting her go for her, not him.

Liar.

"That's harsh." Her hurt punched through him, each realization of what he was doing an arrow sinking into its target.

"That's life for you. Too bad, so sad. Jess the survivor will take it from here. If I can figure out a bus schedule at ten and how to cook and get myself to school, I can survive one asshole who told me, in so many ways, that I wasn't good enough."

"That's not…" he began and then stuttered to a halt. He had said he didn't make a habit of lying and couldn't do so now.

"Bullshit. Fuck off, Kai." She whirled on her heel and stalked across the room as he watched. He made no effort to stop her as she made it to the front door and yanked it open. Then she was outside as the door clicked shut behind her.

Their brief affair was over.

Kai stood in place, fighting to keep from bolting

after her. He had to respect what she demanded. He'd savaged her enough. He listened to her car start, then the soft squeal of protesting tires as she backed out of his driveway. Then did he go to the window and push back the blinds. As he watched, she went down the road and then vanished around the corner to the main street beyond, mingling with the thick traffic.

She was gone.

Standing alone in his empty house, Kai wondered what the hell he had just done.

Chapter Nineteen

An insistent buzzer woke Jess. She punched her pillow and tried to ignore the ringing of their bell. She had nobody she wanted to talk to. When it continued, she forced herself to lurch out of bed and rise. Michelle was still sleeping, and whoever was hassling them this early on a weekday hadn't woken her yet. One of them should be allowed to sleep. Of the two, Michelle had to get to the office, but Jess did not.

The light on her phone blinked with new messages. To her shock, she had ten texts and over twenty missed calls. In addition, her social media notifications dinged. So many different things were happening she couldn't make sense of them.

The bell rang again, and she grabbed her mobile and headed for the front. Michelle stirred in her bedroom, the sheets rustling.

Jess shut her roommate's door and hurried to the intercom. "Who is it?"

"Oh good. Jess, it's Ally. Let me up. We have to talk."

She buzzed Ally up, flipped the lock, and eased the door open. Then she busied herself in the kitchen, starting coffee and putting dishes away. She was nervous, the odd events straining an equilibrium she thought she'd started to regain.

A month had gone by since Shatter Sound released

her and she and Kai separated. She had taken the time to regroup, lick her wounds, and hide from the world. She was unsure why Ally was showing up at this hour, on a workday no less, but that plus the messages didn't bode well. She began to check her phone, but before she could complete the action, Ally pushed into the apartment.

She was dressed in office-appropriate attire of black slacks and a button-down shirt, but her hair was still wet. She didn't have on any makeup, making Jess think that Ally had dropped what she was doing to come to Jess.

Jess' notifications went off again, and she started at the sound, dread crawling over her skin.

"Sorry, it's an inhuman time, and I barged in here unannounced. It's been too long—I should have called before now. Did you…have you checked your phone? The internet? What's happening out there…" Ally trailed off, her lips twisting on unspoken words.

Jess shook her head, her stomach churning. "Is it Kai? Has something happened to him?"

That wouldn't make sense, given her brother's was more than one of the text messages. She'd blurted out the first thing on her mind—and her worst fear.

Ally made a motion that suggested uncertainty. "This isn't about Kai. Last I was told, he was fine, though he's fallen off the radar, so I'm not sure. It's your parents."

"Them? They haven't bugged me in weeks. I assumed they got the message that I wasn't going to bail them out of whatever fictitious scrape they'd gotten themselves into. They stopped calling when word got out the label had dropped me. That was all I needed."

Anger and disgust warred over Ally's features. Jess hadn't kept up with Ally the way she meant to after

Shatter Sound released her, but she had been told through the grapevine that her suspicions about Ally and Dirk hadn't been off base. Dirk Roberts was gone, and Ally promoted into his slot.

"They haven't called in weeks because…check your phone." Ally nodded to the cell sitting on the counter.

Jess grabbed it and unlocked it. She ignored the alerts from Ally since she had the real-life version in front of her. The first text she checked was from Rocky.

—*Call me. It's urgent.*—

She glanced at Ally, whose jaw was clenched, but she said nothing.

She had several calls and texts from random numbers she didn't recognize, plus ones from her manager and Ally. Jess scanned for any messages from Kai, but there were none.

She shouldn't have expected any.

"Why don't you just tell me what's happened?"

Jess poured herself some coffee and held the pot up to Ally, who nodded.

She'd have to apologize later. Right now, nerves were surging through Jess at whatever was happening.

Ally drew in a breath and blew on the steaming brew before taking a sip. "They didn't stop calling because they got the message. They went online to complain when you didn't give them satisfaction. They found some wronged parents' site and posted that you were ignoring them and were letting them go hungry and homeless. They didn't name you outright but dropped enough clues that some guy pieced it together and outed you on the forum. That's why everything is crashing down."

Jess' hand shook when she lifted the coffee cup to

her lips. "I didn't think they knew how to use the internet, never mind find their way to forums. Hold on, let me get my head around this."

The social media notifications showed the worst of the damage. The barrage of hate was horrendous. Some were on her side, but most were calling her a terrible daughter, a stuck-up rock star…and worse. She had some direct messages that suggested she kill herself—in many ways, some inventive, some not so much. Panic warred with anger and hurt, and Jess blinked to stave off the tears that threatened.

"That's a lot." She didn't dare say any more. She cleared her throat and fought for calm.

"I'm sorry." Ally, like Jess, appeared to be at a loss for words.

Michelle's door opened, and she crossed through the hallway.

Jess cleared her throat. "Hey, Michelle, you may consider staying off social media for a while. There's some stuff up with me, and it might get out of control. I can't stop it."

Michelle waved a hand. "That crap always fades in time. The internet is the equivalent of yesterday's newspaper in the bird cage. Don't worry about it."

When she was gone again, Jess fixed on Ally. "How bad is it? I'm nobody now. No record deal, no tour, nothing but songs I don't own and an uncertain future. I'm not anyone the masses care about. Why am I in the spotlight?"

Ally took a sip of coffee. Jess suspected she was using it as a way to delay answering the question. As she waited, more message notifications came in. Rocky again, her manager, and a bunch of unidentified numbers.

"People love a scandal, and that's you. I suggest you lock down your social media right away. Delete your accounts or make them private. This has gone viral, and it will get worse before it gets better."

Jess gestured to the computer in a corner of the living room. "I will. Do you need to go? I don't want to hold you up."

Ally snorted. "I don't care if I'm late. Gordon has already done his worst. I'm under contract now. Fire me, and he has to pay me out."

That was a change for the driven woman. "If you say so."

"I do. Let me help get you fixed up. I had all your social media accounts when we were working together. I brought the list with me. I have to make sure you're covered, and then I'll head for the office. Gordon can wait."

Jess would have laughed if she had any humor in her. "I figured it wasn't my business, but something clearly happened. Will you share, or is it not my concern?"

Shadows lurked on Ally's face. "The short version is that Dirk and I were involved, Gordon found out, tried to fire me, and Dirk quit instead. He's gone, from California and from my life. Gordon had to make me VP to fill the gap. This was happening when we came to see you, but I couldn't say anything."

Jess whistled. "Sorry Dirk didn't stay. Sounds like a man. The job title is well deserved."

Ally made a dismissive gesture with her hand. "It's for a year, and that's all. I took it to keep things stable while I explored my options. When my contract is up,

I'm not going to stay. I need this time, and Gordon owes me that much." She pointed to the computer. "Let's get this done. I'll be better once it is."

The urge to call Rocky was burning in Jess' mind, but she did as Ally asked. Within minutes, everything was set to private. When she did the last one and Ally marked it off her list, Ally met Jess' gaze.

"There's an upside."

Michelle emerged with her purse and made her way out the door to her day job. Jess watched her go.

When the door closed, she glanced at Ally. "What's that?"

Ally went to the computer and called up one of the most popular music sites. She clicked to the top songs and pointed. "You're trending."

Jess blinked. "Susan the Magician" showed at number twelve, something she hadn't achieved the entire time she'd been promoting the album. Under different circumstances, the placement would make her dance.

Now she was just sad—and defeated.

"I bet that will make Gordon happy. He still has all the rights. Thanks for coming, Ally. You should get to work, and I've got a bunch of calls to return."

Ally patted Jess on the shoulder. "Call me if you need me. Hang in there. As your roommate said with a lot more style, this will blow over."

No sooner had Ally left than Jess called Rocky. He picked up before the first ring ended, showing he was waiting by the phone.

"Jess, thank God. Are you okay? My computer is blowing up. I had it set to notify me with information about you, but I never expected this."

She drew in a shuddering breath. "I'm not fine,

Rocky. This is all too much. Can I come for a visit?" He'd always said she could ask him for anything, but offering and opening his home to an intruder were two different things. Everyone let her down in the end.

"Whatever you need. The guesthouse is available. We'd love it if you did."

Her heart lifted. "Thanks, big bro."

"Any time. We'll get the place ready. Text me when you're on your way so I have a time frame for your arrival. I love you."

"Love you back." Though the words didn't come easy to her, she spoke them anyway.

She'd call her manager as she was driving. Jess removed all notification reminders for her accounts and went to pack a bag.

****

When the knocking kept coming, Kai woke. His phone showed eight o'clock. He had no idea who was at the door. Unlike many of his friends, he didn't have outside cameras.

His heart surged. Maybe the person was Jess. He put on a pair of sweatpants and ran for the door.

When he opened it, he tried to suppress disappointment. Clarke Masters stood there, dressed in jeans and a loose T-shirt. Kai had nothing to say to Jess anyway. He was foolish to think that she would return after the way he drove her off. They were over.

He had never felt less like company. He had no Jess to soothe his wounded spirit when he was low. Nobody to bolster his ego and tell him how great he was when his faith faltered.

The gleam of Clarke's wedding ring reminded Kai of all the things he would never have. Love, companionship, children. Jess' children.

He gestured to the living room. "Why don't you come in? Though I can't imagine what you have to say to me."

Clarke moved inside and shut the door behind them before speaking. His tread sounded loud on the polished floor, the echo ominous. "I'm guessing you either don't follow Jessica Baker or haven't been online."

Hearing her name on someone else's lips reminded Kai of their last time, here in this room. He met Clarke's clear green gaze and shook his head. "I'm taking a break from the internet. I have no need to be on it right now." He left out that he might be tempted to check for news of Jess if he did. Better to leave that alone. Instead, he'd done a great deal of meditation and exercise and tried not to contemplate his empty future.

Perhaps he'd take a trip to Hawaii. He could visit family and reconnect. It had been... Kai couldn't remember when he'd last been there.

A woman had been at his self-defense classes, making little secret of her interest. She was perfect for him. She'd already informed him she volunteered at an animal shelter and was a member of Greenpeace and the Sierra Club as well as a vegetarian. She was a slender, pretty brunette in her thirties and the kind of woman he should grab and hold on to. She was everything he was searching for—or had believed he was until Jessica Baker came along.

"I am guessing a certain singer has something to do with that," Clarke said. "Ally and Terri talk, and I get pieces. Why don't you call her? Especially now."

"It's over," Kai responded. "It was a mistake from the start. She made it clear the last time I was out of her life and I need to stay there. But what do you mean by 'especially now'?"

Clarke motioned to the living room. "The story broke days ago. It's all over the internet. You have no idea?"

Kai swallowed and shook his head. The blond man reached over and grasped Kai's shoulder.

"What happened?"

"She's fine—it's nothing physical. She's gone quiet on social media after taking all her profiles private or deleting them. Ally was the last person to be with her, from what I understand."

"What. Happened?"

Clarke gestured to the laptop. "Easier to show you."

Kai shifted from foot to foot as Clarke booted up his computer and surfed until he found what he was after. The air around them crackled with anticipation.

Or perhaps that was him.

As he waited, he checked his phone. Nothing from Jess or Ally, though this had something to do with Shatter Sound. Even if Ally hadn't pinged him, Kai would have expected Terri to reach out, to warn him.

Then again, she'd sent her husband, and that was better than any call.

Clarke turned the computer to him.

Kai stared at the website. "What is this? A forum for parents and their estranged children? Why?"

"Read." Clarke thrust the laptop into Kai's grip. After reading as many posts as he could stomach, he understood. Jess' father had gone onto the forum after Jess continued to ignore his calls. He'd posted that his "rich, successful musician daughter, who had been given everything" had refused to help in their time of need and they had nowhere to turn. That they were going to lose their home because of her selfishness. He had gotten tons of responses from similar-minded parents, calling the mystery child colorful names that made Kai blanch. He could read between the lines, even if Clarke hadn't directed him to the site, and follow the clues to determine that the singer being spoken about was Jess.

More than one had done so. Several posts down was a post saying, "Is this the one?" with a picture identifying Jess.

"How bad is it?" Kai considered closing the device but kept it open. He glanced at Clarke, who waved at the screen.

"Before she took her profiles private, Jess was getting bombarded by hate mail. That's what Ally said. Most think she's a selfish, self-involved, narcissistic artist who used her parents and abandoned them when she got famous."

Kai's fingers clenched hard on the laptop, and his knuckles went white. He put it down and stood, his breath laboring under the force of his emotions. "That's so far from the truth it's not funny."

Clarke snorted. "You know the net, man. If it's posted, it must be true."

Words danced in his mind, bits of memory crowding his thoughts. He cast a sideways glance at Clarke. "You said she's gone?"

"Vanished. Poof. She's somewhere but isn't saying where. I bet you could find her."

"I can't. I shouldn't."

"Of course you should. She's hurt and hiding. You ought to reach out for her sake. Maybe she'll take your calls."

Kai shook his head. "When she left me, she said not to call. I will honor that. I owe her."

Clarke made a disgusted sound. "And you're going to listen?"

Kai shot him an angry glare. "Don't go rock star on me. You've grown up since your selfish days. I respect her and her wishes." A terrible chaotic energy washed over him. Jessica, *his* Jessica, was being brutalized online, and he'd had no idea. She was wounded, in pain, and—he had no right to help her.

"This is the guy who walked into Terri's apartment and told her to go fight for me? That she shouldn't let me go? You're telling me that what you said about us doesn't apply to you?"

Kai gritted his teeth to stop from shouting. "Just because you have found the light of your life doesn't mean everyone is so fortunate. What was good for you and Terri is not for me and Jessica. I'm ten years older than her and from a different world. The whole idea is ridiculous."

"Nobody's going to care when she's sixty-five and you're seventy-five. It's bullshit, Kai."

"Bullshit or not, it's over. She's too good for me."

"She sure is, but I'm betting she doesn't see things the same way."

Kai opened his mouth to challenge the statement but instead just rocked back on his heels and accepted the condemnation.

Clarke sighed when Kai said nothing. "Stay away from her if she means nothing to you, man. I have an opinion about that if you do. It involves you being a damned fool."

Kai took several deep breaths to bring his pulse back

to normal. Clarke waited, studying his old friend before speaking.

"I'm going to tell you something." Clarke pushed him in the chest. "I had three days thinking things were over with me and Terri. Three days thinking I'd lost the one woman for me. I aged a lifetime in those seventy-two hours. Imagine living the rest of your years on this planet without the woman you love. She's hurting, man, and she needs you."

Kai ripped away from Clarke before the man could detect his blazing emotions written all over his face. He couldn't face his friend's gaze anymore. "I should stay away."

Clarke put his hand on Kai's back. "Remember what you told me and think about what your next right course of action is."

Kai hung his head. "I said I'd leave her alone, and I have to honor it. If I don't, then I'm no better than the monsters who did this to her online."

Clarke snorted. "If you believe that, then you are an idiot. I've done all I can do. I promised Terri I'd try."

Kai inhaled a ragged breath. "Tell her thanks. Terri has always been a wise woman, whether she was aware of her power or not."

Clarke held out his hand, and Kai took it. Then Clarke pulled Kai into an embrace. "You were there for me when I was down. You need anything, say the word."

An idea began forming in Kai's head. He glanced to the computer and then back at Clarke. "I will. Right now, there's something I have to do."

Clarke nodded and clapped Kai on the shoulder. "Make it good."

After Clarke left, Kai yanked the laptop to him.

Ideas swirled in his head, a thousand different notions competing for space. He was a man at loose ends, with no job and little idea of what he was going to do next. He'd been relieved he didn't get the Plausive gig, telling him that a return to an office was not his future. When they called and said they'd gone with their second candidate, he'd almost danced. His suspicion that Gordon had gotten to them and persuaded them not to hire him didn't negate his relief at not being given the position. A different road tugged at his consciousness, one he was still formulating.

But right now—Jess. He'd maintain his distance, as promised, but that wasn't the sole action he could take. He had it in his power to fix things. She didn't deserve what was happening to her, not the kind, wonderful woman who had done nothing more than do what was necessary to survive.

The memory of the day when Jess had created that beautiful tune that had been lurking in her subconscious until it burst forth flooded him. The raw, emotional song was the best thing she'd written because the sentiments were true to who she was and not the persona she imagined the public sought from her. The person in that video was the real Jess. It showed her vulnerability without words. This was the woman who could set the world on fire. This one, the Jess whose emotions went right to the core of her—the ones she tried to hide.

He could change things. All he needed to do was act.

Kai was aware that he should ask her first but couldn't be sure he wouldn't just be making excuses to get in contact with her. He owed her his silence—and this.

He still had his memories. He had that video and the

pain and passion her pure, bright song showed. The memory of the injustice done to her danced inside her. Kai had all that.

He had something more. A mission.

Chapter Twenty

"Knock, knock." Her brother's voice sounded through the door before he poked his head in.

Rocky's detached one-room guesthouse located at the back of the property suited her just fine. She had all the freedom she needed and access to his family on everyone's own terms.

Life would have been good, except for the hole in her heart.

"Hiya, Rocky." The scent of coffee and bacon wafted in with him. "You brought me breakfast. My hero."

His familial resemblance was in the shape of his jaw and facial structure, though he was taller and broader. He set the tray down, poured some coffee, and handed it to her. "Morning, sis. Vanessa is asking if you will help her with music lessons sometime today. I said I'd find out."

Jess noted that he didn't suggest anything outside of the house. She hadn't left the safety of his yard since she'd gotten there. She'd have to, in time.

Not yet.

"I'm always happy to do that. She's up already?"

He grunted out a laugh and poured some coffee for himself. "Not a chance. Never before nine when she's not in school. She asked me last night before we went to bed. I'd appreciate it. She loves her aunt Jess helping her, but that's because you're you and not me. She's like you were at that age—independent to a fault."

Jess grabbed a slice of bacon and nibbled on it. "The difference is that she doesn't have to clean up Dad's puke or step around him if he's passed out in the hallway. I had to be self-sufficient. She chooses to be."

"True. Anything I need to be aware of on that front? Our folks, I mean?"

She shook her head, her attention going to her tablet. "I haven't been online since the day I left a note for my roommate and got out of Los Angeles. I don't have to be told what's being said. Random internet strangers can have all the opinions in the world about me, but I don't have to read them. Taking a break from social media is doing me good. I've got enough songs for a new album, if I had someone to produce it."

He let out a breath that was shadowed by old hurts, echoed in her memories. "I could learn, if you need an engineer. I'm good with machines."

She wouldn't tell anyone that she also couldn't get on her email in case she weakened and sent a note to Kai. He hadn't called, and that was its own answer. He would honor his word. He had vanished from her life as she had asked. He was so gone Kai Halara might never have existed, if not for the ache in her soul.

"You're a sweetheart, but you've done plenty already. I can't ask for more. Still quiet on the troll front? They haven't tracked you down?"

Rocky set the mug down. He sprawled into the single chair next to the twin mattress and gave her a piercing stare. "Our folks tried to toss me under the bus too, which I expected. They posted on that forum that you had a terrible older brother who also abandoned them the minute he could leave home and refused to give them money. They claim to be this close to being out on the street, but the house is paid off. I've checked into the deed."

"Unless they took out a second mortgage to fund their lifestyle."

He pointed to a slice of bacon, and she motioned for him to go ahead. The times that they'd been engaged in over the last few weeks were soothing her wounded soul. Rocky wasn't Kai, but he was family. Kai was a fantasy, her brother the reality. The sooner she released Kai, the better.

"Possible. Also not our concern. They parentified you, Jess, and you still have those instincts. Don't let them get to you. The idea of me as the evil sibling didn't get as much traction because I'm not in the public awareness. I'm handling it. If this gets worse and engulfs my wife and kid, I'll act. I won't allow anything to happen to Vanessa."

"You're a gem."

"Far from it. I wish I'd done more when you were a kid. This is my way of making up for it. You blocked Mom and Dad, right? We have."

She nodded, and he held out his arms. She went into his embrace, holding her older brother close.

Things were going to be okay.

Later, Jess plugged her guitar into her amp and routed it through her headphones so she alone could hear it. Bending to the instrument, she played through the sheet music she'd written out, although she didn't need the writing to remind her. Again and again, she ran through the song, her callused fingers repeating the notes until she had them memorized, noting changes as she went, and also recording the changes to a four-track recorder.

This nightmare had been good for something. Now that she had no future to aspire to, her muse had struck with a vengeance.

When her creativity petered out, Jess put down her guitar and took a quick shower before donning a T-shirt and drawstring pants. Then she padded across the yard to the sliding glass door in the back and let herself inside.

Jess was met by Vanessa bounding to her with a big grin on her face.

"Aunt Jess, you have to come. It's incredible."

The only people in the house at this time were her and Vanessa, who had her tablet held out in front of her. Rocky would be home later, and Elaine was running errands. The two of them were alone. At this age, Vanessa didn't need a babysitter, but Jess tried to keep an eye out anyway—unobtrusively, she hoped.

"What's going on?" Jess didn't approach the computer. She hadn't missed the internet since she unplugged. Perhaps that was what accounted for her burst of creativity. She should do it more often.

"You have to see. It's crazy."

Jess had no desire to check into what was being said about her. The freedom from not having to endure the toxicity of strangers made her wonder if she would ever go back to public life. Maybe she'd become a songwriter and sell her stuff on the open market. That way she could keep away from the media and still do what she loved.

That alternative was something to consider. She might never get the rights back to the song on her Shatter Sound album, but she could continue to create new ones.

"I'm taking a break from the internet." She tried not to sound angry. Teenagers were sensitive, and they weren't so far apart in age that she didn't recall what life was like at thirteen.

Her niece's tablet was a mishmash of apps, from the latest bands to her favorite online influencers. The way hers might have been if she'd been allowed to grow up the way Vanessa had. Then again, if she had been given a normal childhood, she might not have so many songs. She couldn't regret what she couldn't change.

"You'll love this. Trust me."

Jess waited as Vanessa found what she was searching for. She wasn't familiar with the sites Vanessa was accessing, but soon recognized one where the public could post videos. Her brows drew together in confusion, and she glanced at Vanessa, but her niece said nothing.

"Vanessa?"

Vanessa pressed a button with a "ta-da" flourish. "Listen. You'll love this."

The last thing she expected was to hear a piece of the song she'd finished that day in Kai's house. She didn't have it written down anywhere besides the video Kai took. After the initial chords, the familiarity of the tune that had haunted her left Jess no doubt this was from that day. Vanessa shoved the tablet in front of her, forcing Jess to pay attention to the screen.

Her face greeted her, and the notes that played through Vanessa's speakers filled her with the same emotions she'd had when she wrote it. Love. Loss. Longing.

The track went through the first verse and the chorus before stopping and repeating. At least not all of it had been released. She supposed she should be thankful for that. She was unaware of anything but the fury bubbling up inside her. Even as her niece hummed along with the chorus, suggesting she'd listened to the clip more than once, the anger didn't abate. This was *hers* and nobody else's.

She had no doubt Kai had done this. He had put her most intimate creation out for the uncaring public online to pick apart. She gazed at her image on the screen and then at Vanessa, who was grinning from ear to ear.

How dare he?

****

Gordon's voice was harsh over the speaker. "Bold move, Halara."

"I'm not clear what you're referring to." He'd debated not taking the call. Kai didn't care what Gordon had to say. He couldn't affect Kai—or Jess. Not anymore.

"Don't play dumb. That video was taken at your house. I recognize it from a party you invited me to. Anything you say would be a lie. Just admit it."

The barb, which Kai was sure what Gordon intended, sank but didn't hook. "I make a point of telling the truth, so yes, I uploaded that snippet. Not all of it, as I didn't want Jess to lose the ability to monetize the full song if she desired. The rest was organic."

Gordon snorted, and Kai could almost picture the redness that crawled over his face as it did when Gordon was pissed.

Not my circus, not my monkeys.

"I'd say you did us a favor, but you fucked us too. We've got no rights to that song. Everyone is clamoring for it. That's what they're after, not the stuff on the album."

Kai flopped onto his sofa and stared at the ceiling. Memories of the last time he and Jessica had made love in this place flooded him. She lurked cross-legged on the floor, strumming his guitar, in his kitchen as she got coffee, in his bed as she called his name…

"From the charts I've found, she's gotten a bounce off your releases. There's a reason her manager ensured you had no rights to anything she did in the future. The best was yet to come." Kai shouldn't have said the words but couldn't resist.

"Fuck you, Halara."

Kai's snort of laughter was loud, and Gordon huffed.

"If Jess were still with the label, you could capitalize on this, but alas, you cannot. All you can do is utilize what you have."

"I could take Jess to court and tie her up."

Kai clenched the cell so tight he was afraid he might break it. "Since you were the ones who dropped her and Jess wasn't the one asking to get out of her deal, I don't think that would go very far."

He made a mental note to call her manager as soon as he was done with Gordon. The man had to be aware of what Gordon was threatening. While he doubted Gordon would succeed, he could delay things.

"I hate failed executives who think they are still relevant."

A thousand responses surged through Kai. He had to resist the urge to throw angry words back at Gordon. All exchanging barbs with someone did was wound the man who threw them. Still, Kai couldn't help but be smug. This was something Gordon could no longer control. Jess was gone, due to Gordon's actions.

"You didn't call me to bandy about—nor to be social. What is on your mind, Gordon?"

Gordon was silent for several seconds and then released a breath. "I'm hoping you have a way to get in touch with Jessica Baker."

"Why?" Kai let the seconds tick by, waiting for Gordon's response.

"You are the smart guy. You're aware of why." His sentences were slow and deliberate, as though Kai had forced them out of him.

Maybe he had. Kai didn't much care. "Of course I do, and the answer is no. Even if I did, I wouldn't tell you. Reach out to her manager or…Ally."

Gordon snorted, a loud exhalation that showed his annoyance. "She won't say, and right now I can't push her. Come on, man, just tell me. We could make a killing off the whole song—release it as a special edition or whatever. You owe me. I gave you work when you were unemployed."

Yes, and I offered you my best, but you didn't listen. "Is that how you see it? I have it on good authority Dirk Roberts left and you promoted Ally. Smart man."

"I had no choice, just like I don't now. Help a guy out. This could do wonders for Jess' career. It's taking off in a way nobody could have anticipated."

A thought struck Kai. He sat upright on the sofa.

Maybe he wasn't a record executive anymore, but he still had his expertise. What had been lurking in his mind now surged through at Gordon's words. Kai had always enjoyed developing artists. That was his best talent, the thing he was famous for. That was what he should be focusing on.

He didn't need to own a label to do what he was good at. In this modern world, many ways existed to get to the same goal. "Jess is taking off no thanks to you."

Gordon sputtered something indistinct. "Why do you have to be like that? Come on, give me this one. I'll give you a job if that's what it takes. I could make you a producer or something else. Dirk's position is open."

Kai snorted. "No, it's not. You promoted the right person, and suggesting anything different is wrong. That's not my skill set, and even if it had been, I'm not for sale. I can't help you, or rather, I won't help you. I have to go. Good luck with…everything."

Kai hung up to the muffled sound of Gordon cursing. He didn't care. Gordon was no longer relevant to anything Kai did. He and his label were part of Kai's past, just as Apposite was. He had a new endeavor to pursue—and he would start with Jessica, if she would have him. He hoped she would. She had to. Jess loved him—didn't she?

He had to go to her. He had to find her and talk to her. He'd done this thing without her permission but didn't think she would mind. Releasing the video clip worked out for the best. She was getting the traction she'd always strived for.

He had shown the world they were wrong about her. She couldn't fault him for that. Jessica Baker was a warm, understanding woman. Revitalizing her career was a bonus. He could work with that—she could capitalize on it.

All he needed was to run this past her. The idea was perfect for her—and him.

Kai understood deep down that he was lying to himself. More than her profession lay in the balance.

Ally would be aware of where Jess was. He was sure of it. If not Ally, then Michelle, her roommate. He would find Jess, whatever it took.

He picked up the phone to call Ally. He had to get to Jess. The ideas that were still forming danced in his mind with the clarity of their promise. This would fix things. All he needed was a chance to convince her.

Her future, and his, depended on that contact.

Chapter Twenty-One

Jess was showing Vanessa chords when the doorbell rang. Rocky went to the door and spoke in low tones, blocking their view of the interior. Jess didn't glance up. Whoever was at the door, the person was either a friend of Rocky's or an unwelcome visitor. Rocky had taken command of the guests coming in and out of the house. She was safe. If a nosy influencer or journalist showed up, her big brother would take care of it.

When Rocky slammed the door behind him, he had a scowl on his face that reminded her of their dad when he was going to launch into one of his tirades.

"Solicitor?"

He shook his head, his attention still fixed on the closed door. "Some Asian guy. Says he's friends with Jess. I told him nobody lived here by that name and to go away. That he wasn't welcome."

Asian guy?

Her heart beating fast, Jess scrolled through her pictures and found one she'd taken of the two of them while on tour. The bad selfie cast his profile in shadow, but his image was clear. "By any chance, is it this guy?"

Rocky glanced at the device and then back to her. "He's not some stranger, then. Should I have been nicer?"

Knocking started on the door again as Jess' notifications dinged with a text from Kai.

—It's me. Please let me in.—

"Yeah, I guess so. We have some unfinished business."

Rocky strode back to the door and opened it. Jess set the guitar down and rose, wiping her hands on her jeans.

Not too long ago she'd have done anything to have Kai chase after her like this. Now all she felt was numb.

"Kai," she mouthed, joining Rocky at the door. She placed a hand on Rocky's shoulder.

He crossed his arms, his chest rising and falling.

"It's okay, Rocky." Her heart started a trip-hammer beat at Kai's presence. "Everyone."

Her entire focus was on the man in front of her.

Lines bracketed his mouth and forehead, ones that hadn't been there a month earlier. His clothes were rumpled, a far cry from his normal neat appearance. He was wearing his glasses, and his hair was pulled back, much as it had been that first time they'd gone out together.

"What are you doing here?"

"I…" He spread his arms in a helpless gesture. "Can we…do you think…do you have time to talk? I'll just take a few minutes."

She had it on the tip of her tongue to refuse, but her heart wouldn't obey.

Rocky's gaze swept over Kai, and a muscle jumped in his jaw. "My sister told me that a 'friend' uploaded that video without her knowing. I am guessing you're that guy? You didn't have the right to do that, however it panned out."

Kai nodded and bowed, just a bob of his head. It didn't placate Rocky, who might be one step from ordering Kai out of the house.

"I did. Her parents, the way the internet was going after her…I couldn't bear it. I was there when she came up with it, and I was positive it would do the job." His gaze was impenetrable when he met her eyes. "I didn't think it through, Jess. I just reacted. Your brother is right. I didn't have permission. I'm sorry for doing that but not that the tune is getting the recognition it deserves."

"Kai, this is my family. Rocky, Elaine, and my niece, Vanessa."

He nodded to them. "Pleasure to meet the best influence in Jess' life. She speaks well of you."

The joy Jess might have once gloried in at the compliment was a dull throb, lying underneath pain and betrayal. "How did you find me? Ally?"

He shook his head. "She wouldn't tell. I had to bribe your roommate and promise her that I meant well. It took some pressure, but she gave in. Don't be mad, Jess. She supposed she was doing the right thing."

She made a mental note to have words with Michelle when she got back to Los Angeles. Then again, she was sure many had tried to get to her and the one person Michelle told had been Kai. Her friend had her reasons.

"How do you know Jessica?" Elaine's voice was careful, in the tone she used when Vanessa had done something wrong.

Jess glanced at her brother's family and couldn't help a goofy grin that slid over her face.

For the first time in her life, she was supported. All the years that had passed when she had to struggle with herself and her wits to get her by, and now she had these around her who cared about her. Even if they were opposed to the man she might still love.

"I was hired to work with Jess and improve her stage

set, among many things. That was all window dressing. Gordon's real agenda—that's the label head if she hasn't mentioned his name—was to find fault with her and dump her from her contract. I refused, in fact suggested ways Gordon could improve her, and that was the end of my time at Shatter Sound. I got to respect her and her talents in that process. We're…friends."

The beginnings of a tune stirred within Jess at Kai's words, something she would focus on soon enough.

"None of that gives you the right to put her video online." Though Elaine's tone was even, Jess had come to be aware of her sister-in-law's moods over the last weeks. She was angry too, perhaps as much as Jess and Rocky. Both of them had her back.

If things weren't so topsy-turvy, Jess would be ecstatic.

"You're correct. I don't regret it." A muscle jumped in Kai's jaw. The living room air was heavy with unspoken undercurrents.

She'd understood Kai was the logical person to have leaked the video, of course, but hearing it put into words emphasized her anger. Her body jerked, and he gave her a quick side-glance.

"That was great. The grands were pissed! They spammed the f…heck out of Dad, trying to get him to get it taken down. Said they looked like monsters and that wasn't fair. As though their crappy lies on that stupid forum hadn't done that already."

Jess made a startled sound as her brother tried to hush his daughter, whose lips curved up in a smile. "Is that true? You didn't tell me."

All the while, Kai stood there, his presence a beacon in the room, drawing her attention. Flickers of differing emotions moved inside her, like fireflies searching for a place to rest.

"No reason to. I handled it. You're here to take a break and recharge, not get sucked into their crazy. We went no contact after that. But yeah, they did try. Stalked all three of us for a day from new numbers before we blocked those too. I talked to them once to tell them the fallout was not in my control and to stop calling. That they had no right to their bad behavior and that you owed them nothing. That they would get nothing from any of us and they had better wise up, or they would never be in the company of any of their grandchildren—Vanessa and any you might have. Dad cursed at me and called me some select names before hanging up."

The interaction made Jess yearn for that emotion from a different man, in his way.

Rocky gave his daughter an affectionate grin. "I am positive you checked, sweetie. How was it on that forum?"

Vanessa's smug look was incandescent. The world was lighter, more tolerable. She had her family, and everything was going to be okay.

Whatever happened with Kai.

"Plenty of users on there still cosign their bull—" Vanessa cut off the last word, her cheeks turning pink.

"Vanessa." Rocky's voice was firm.

"Stuff. They loved it when Jess was first outed, and ate up all the posts saying what a terrible daughter she was. They didn't like it when the video went viral and the members of the site went for them, asking if they had been those kinds of parents. They vanished after the board got filled with folks now claiming that they were horrid and Jess owed them nothing." Vanessa shifted and shrugged. "It got boring after that."

Kai focused on Jess. "You are trending. This clip is all over the music services and charting. You could say it's your revenge."

A million splintered emotions danced inside her even as Vanessa whooped in appreciation.

"I didn't write the song for payback. I wrote it because I had to." Jess' tone was cold, and she didn't change it. Her days of tiptoeing around Kai's needs were over.

She wasn't the same person she had been when she walked out of his house all those weeks ago. She had assumed she wouldn't forget when that had happened, but she had. Time didn't care. The clock would move no matter what she did. All she could do was live and go forward.

Kai's lips twitched, but his face remained impassive. "Of course. You wouldn't be you if things were different. Jessica, can I speak to you? In private?"

Rocky's growl filled the room.

"Yes." She met Rocky's gaze, and he said nothing further. "I'm staying in the guesthouse. We can talk there."

****

The walk across the lawn might as well have been a thousand miles. Kai hadn't been sure what he'd been expecting when he showed up at the house, but this reserved, unreadable Jessica wasn't it. Her brother's protection he expected and liked, but he'd believed Jess would be more welcoming. He had gotten so used to Jess' warmth that the stranger in her place was unnerving.

He leaned by the closed door, taking in the one-room guest space that had no touch of Jessica except the second guitar in its stand and a scattering of music paper next to it. He tucked his hands in his pockets, gazing at her from under lowered brows.

"Kai, why are you here?" she asked.

All the fantasies he'd had about her throwing herself into his arms evaporated in the afternoon air. Raising his head, he started pacing, short bursts back and forth.

He stopped again and faced her head-on. "I had so many reasons for letting you go. I was a man adrift, not having any clue about what I did next. I told myself you should be focusing on your career. I was ten years older and had already proven I could fail. I wasn't in the market for love, not until I got back on my feet, and not with a woman like you."

She flinched, and he wished he could take back the reminder. Birds chirped in the trees in the yard, but all he could think of were the discordant chords of their unspoken words. Hurt and pain moved between them, as real as the dust motes visible in the rays of light coming through the window.

"Why are you here now?"

He swayed, searching for the right combination of syllables to convince this woman of his truth. "I told myself that I couldn't tie us together when I had nothing to offer you. You said you loved me, but I didn't have the ability to hold you to that."

"Damn it, Kai!" Jess cried, her voice desperate and rough. "You are dodging the fuck out of my questions. Why did you think you had the right to post the video after you dumped me? Why did you track me down? Why. Are. You. Here? We said everything we had to say that day. I told you I loved you. You were like, yeah, that's nice. I left. That was that. Until now."

A thousand things danced through his mind. "You keep your emotions under wraps unless pushed. This is a nice change, though it's directed at me."

She snorted in an indelicate sound. He couldn't help but notice the way the sun played off her hair and face, making her shine. She was a light—his light.

The one he had thrown away.

"Welcome to the new Jess. I'm still learning who I am, but having hundreds of internet strangers condemn me as a jerk and then more come to my defense has been enlightening. More than that, being here with my brother and Elaine has shown that if someone loves me, they are there for me. Rocky and his family showed me the difference."

You did not. The words were unspoken but sank into him like a raptor ripping through his skin and grabbing his heart. He had done this. To her and to himself.

A shadow flew across the window and his soul. He understood too late what he'd tossed aside. She had given of herself again and again until she had nothing left. A part of him had always assumed she'd be there for whenever he got his head out of his rear end and contacted her. Now here he was, and she wasn't welcoming him. Quite the reverse. Her folded arms, the set coldness to her face, told him that his visit was not just unexpected but unwelcome.

"You deserve that, and you deserved better. From your parents"—*may as well rip the bandage off*—"and from me."

Jess' face remained stony. Her gaze bounced from him to the yard outside. He wondered if her protective kin was waiting on the far side of the sliding glass door, ready to eject him if she said the word.

He was pretty sure the answer was yes.

"I tried so hard, Kai. I believed if I could just find the right combination of you and me, we could be more. You touched me with such passion I allowed myself to believe that it had to be more than sex. I was kidding myself, just as I had with my folks. I can't change anyone, and I shouldn't twist into some sort of pretzel over who I think they need me to be. That's not love. I'm not even sure what to name it anymore."

All his dreams were crumbling to dust in front of him, and he had no way to stop the destruction. Kai let out a low moan and rocked back on his heels.

He had ruined everything.

"I…" He tried to speak, but no words came.

"Why did you release the video? That was a private song, and I wasn't ready to share it with the world."

She was relentless, pressing each of his failings home until the shattered remnants of his fantasies pierced his insides. He tasted the ashes of failure and defeat. He had lost a prize he should have cherished.

Moisture gathered in his soul, but he would not give in to the luxury of tears. He'd done this to himself and would pay the price. "No amount of folks defending you, including me, Ally, half the strangers online, would convince those who were reading these forums for kicks of the truth. That beautiful, haunting reminiscence about your childhood, and the strength it took to endure what you went through, would. I didn't have your permission, and for that I'm sorry. I'm not sorry for posting it, though. It's a gorgeous song and shows who you are better than anything else could, including everything on your first album. It's real and raw and amazing. Like you."

She let out a slow exhale and shifted her attention back to the window. They were in the same room but might as well have been a hundred miles apart. He could have stayed in Los Angeles for all the impact his being here was having. She was there in body, but her mind was far away. She'd cataloged and shelved him, put him in the wastebasket of her history and moved on. She'd taken his rejection to heart and accepted it. Like she had been doing all her life. All that took a toll, though. Her emotions were the price.

She had stopped loving him.

Kai had lost the greatest gift he'd ever been offered, all because he'd been scared. He had the love that Clarke had spoken about handed to him and, in his blind stupidity, had cast what Jess offered into the abyss. Now that he understood his mistake, he couldn't go back. He'd waited too long.

They were over.

He didn't have any idea how he was going to bear it.

Chapter Twenty-Two

She could do this. All she had to do was stay strong.

She was Jessica Baker and didn't grovel for anyone. Not for this man, whom she had begged to love her, and he had flat out told her no. That Jessica Baker hadn't been good enough for him. This one was someone new.

"I'm mad you didn't ask for permission, but you have a point. The album I did for Shatter Sound was good, but it wasn't real. It skipped on the surface, trying to be witty and not letting folks in. That's not what an artist does. The authentic Jess Baker is messy and complicated with a shitty childhood and a confused adulthood. New Jessica is all about being my true self. I might never have had the courage to release that song, so I owe you for that."

His gaze was so dark he might as well be part of the night, even in the bright midday sunshine. "You'll forgive me for overstepping?"

She scrunched up her face before nodding. "For that, yes." She laughed. "Vanessa showed me the music services. It's doing well. I'm going to have to record a real version and put it out somehow. But not with Shatter Sound. Maybe not with any label. Artists don't need one these days."

"No. They don't."

His agreement didn't soothe her jagged edges. She waited for some reaction, something besides his usual impossible-to-read aura. Kai hadn't changed. He was still the same impassive man he'd been when they first met that she'd been so fascinated with she engineered him going on tour with her. That had precipitated...all this, for better or worse.

He took a step to her and then stopped. "I didn't imagine this was how things would play out. I still have a pillow that has your scent on it. I haven't been able to wash it. That was the last thing I had of yours, except bittersweet memories."

A month ago, his words would have made her dance with joy. Now she couldn't find the right emotion.

"You gave me a precious gift, of yourself and your heart, and I tossed it away. I used age and your profession as an excuse, but I was aware of what I was doing. I was scared to face the truth of the depth of my feelings. You were special right from the start, and I was the one who lacked the courage to face that. I wasn't honest with either one of us."

"Kai..." Her throat closed, and she couldn't say anything further. Struggling to stave off tears, she took note of the bleakness in his posture when she remained motionless. The savage part of her was glad for that hurt.

"I thought that nothing could be worse than losing my company. I'd dreamed of my own label for my whole life. Having it fail brought the world down around my ears." He stared at her, his chest heaving with emotion. "I was wrong. Driving you off, throwing your love away, was the most painful thing in my life. I told myself it would get easier, but each day without you is like moving through quicksand."

She would not cry. She could not cry. "Do you think I give a damn about anyone else? What their opinions were? I've been laughed at behind my back all my life. I'm the child of messed-up alcoholic parents, and that tainted me. Then I was the stupid girl who pursued a career as a country singer. I was the woman who wasn't good enough to love, not for the long term. That didn't change with you. I don't understand what you're trying to say. I said I loved you, and you threw it back at me like it meant nothing. Like I meant nothing. I learn my lessons, Kai, and I don't need to be told twice."

She stood where she was as he came closer until they were face-to-face.

"I understand how badly I messed up, believe me. You gave me everything, and I didn't appreciate the gift. Jessica, this, your song, I can help you with that. I recognize I'm too late for the rest, but not to make a difference in your career." His voice was flat, the words toneless. "I've given a lot of consideration to what I do next, and I won't go back to a label. Plausive didn't hire me, and I was grateful. I can guide artists' careers without the restriction of a company. That's my skill set, and it's what I have always been good at. Let me start with you. We can record the songs I am sure you've been writing, and I will handle the rest. You don't have to pay me a dime until you take off. I doubt that will take long. Call it my way of making it up to you."

She gazed up at him, a flicker of confusion surging through her. "This is all happening too fast. What are you talking about?"

Movement behind the curtains in the main house told her that her family was keeping tabs on them. Her brother would be there if she needed him.

Kai backed up a step, and she was glad of whatever pain she'd caused. He'd done worse, a thousand times over.

"You. Your career. I have this idea. Anyone can create content and upload it on a hundred different sites. The challenge is to cut through the clutter and get your music noticed. That's where I come in. I've got the talent and the business skills to get a person elevated above the rest. I didn't understand what my next move was until I put your song out there. Then when it took off, it all became clear to me. The concept has been bubbling under my consciousness for some time, and then it sprang forth. I can help you, Jess. We can't get back your recorded songs, but we can create new ones. That's what I will do—for you. Consider it payment on my debt of being a jerk to you. I owe you this."

A million hurtful barbs went through Jess' mind, both to him and to herself. She inhaled, tasting bitterness and Kai's scent in that movement. "What makes you think I want that from you?"

****

Kai rocked back on his heels. He recognized karma when it bit him, and he'd just been dished a healthy dose.

He'd done this to her and to himself, and he understood what the proper thing to do was. *Get out, leave her alone, and stay out of her life.*

She gestured to the sheet music. "I've written a dozen songs since I've been here. The quiet helps me to think. My brother and sister-in-law are all the family I ever could have imagined. My one regret is that I didn't come here sooner. I believed that I was after the rock-star life, the touring and the fans and the adulation, but all that gets me is empty hours on the road and a shitty hotel room to put my head in until it's time to head out again, if I'm not sleeping in my bus. That was the life I had signed up for, but the truth is that's not for me. The tour with Ryder was fun because I was with Ryder—and you. I had a better time writing songs in your living room than I did waking up not knowing what state I was in."

He blew out a breath. His entire world had been snatched from him, but she was still talking. Kai tried to focus on what she was saying, but all he could do was try to stand straight and not be swamped by the despair threatening to double him over. She didn't love him anymore. He'd killed that with his actions. His karma had come to roost.

"Touring is part of being a musician, but not the way it used to be. Things are much more fluid now. I've done my research. Some, like Shatter Sound, cling to an old business model, but smart businesses adapt. I likely would have done similar but didn't have enough time." How could he be speaking when his world was crumbling? He should be getting out of there to go back to the airport and fly home to his empty house and emptier life.

He had destroyed everything and had to stand there and take it. He'd earned that. He would do it, for Jess' sake. He would leave her better than she came in, even if he'd already done so much to damage her. He had himself to blame—he couldn't put this on anyone else. She had always been the woman for him. She'd understood it when he didn't—or refused to.

Too late. Too late. The drumbeat of regret echoed in his mind.

"And you'd do that for me? Just because?"

So many words. None he should say. He had no right to inflict this on her. She'd made her choice, and if he was who he was supposed to be, he would honor that.

"I'd do that for you because you deserve it. You weren't given any breaks and fought for everything you earned. Shatter Sound shouldn't have signed you without having a better plan for what to do with you. Losing Dirk didn't help. Ally is amazing at what she does, but she's not a marketing person. You were always a fish out of water there. Gordon did you a favor. Now you can be who you're supposed to be. Write your songs, and I'll get them in front of the public. Even if you deal with me through your manager and we don't have direct contact, I accept that. I did that, and I am a man who believes in owning up to his karma. No matter the rules you lay down, I'll still help you. Let me do this, Jess, for what we should have been and for what you could be. I owe you that."

"Goddamn it, Kai."

He waited, watching the play of emotions over her face. So many slid over her expressive countenance that he couldn't name them all. But he was sure one was buried that he wouldn't have the privilege of indulging in again. Love. He'd destroyed that by being a stubborn, pigheaded tool.

She moved back from him, colliding with the guitar stand. She steadied it with a shaking hand before focusing on him again. "I have no idea what you want me to say."

He had to stay and do this. For both of them. He owed it to her to hear her out. "Say whatever you need to. I was wrong, and I am sorry for what I did. That can't make up for what happened, but it's the truth."

He waited, but she didn't speak. His spirits sank. He'd gotten as low as he could until he threw away the best thing that ever happened to him and tried to get her back.

With no success, if he wasn't mistaken.

"You have so much to offer the world. You're a beautiful woman, a gifted artist, and a wonderful human being. I didn't think I had the right to ask you to be with me, no matter that I loved you beyond all rational thought. I love you like fire, Jess. Without you I am half a soul."

****

She snorted out a breath. "You've got to be kidding me. You come here to throw that at me now? After everything that went down? You were all that mattered. I loved you, and I wasn't subtle about it, just like I tried to get my folks to give a shit. They didn't, and neither did you."

He huffed out a sigh and ducked his head, dark strands falling across his face. "I deserved that, though the comparison stings. I told myself you were better off without me and I was doing this for you. I was arrogant, and all I can say is I'm sorry. I threw away a precious gift, one beyond measure. I'll regret it for a long time to come. You'll never know how much."

Jess pierced him with a glare. "Why?"

He blinked and frowned. "What do you mean?"

Hope beat inside her like fragile wings emerging from a cocoon. "You said two things. That you loved me and also that I'd never know how much you regretted throwing me away. Which is it?"

He sputtered and held out his hands in front of him. "I don't understand."

"You love me?"

He nodded, the gesture spasmodic. "My philosophy teaches that we are all searching for the person who completes us. You are that. It scares the hell out of me."

She reached out and smacked him hard across the chest. "You asshole."

The color drained out of his face, and she was savagely glad.

"You complete and utter asshole. You walked away from me and let me believe you didn't love me? Then you waltz in here thinking you can throw my career at me as a way to get me back? You say you love me pretty damned easily—now. Where were you a month ago? Longer? I can't—no, I won't—be jacked around. Not again, and not by you."

Her words must have registered because Kai flinched but remained still. "You're right, in everything you say. All I can reiterate is I am sorry."

Mixed emotions danced through her mind. She'd been shown the brass ring so many times and had it snatched away. "You pushed me to the side and left me there. I was done, I thought."

Kai uttered a low, despairing cry and drew back. Sorrow etched his face into harsh lines, but before he could turn away, Jess stopped him with a hand on his arm.

"I should hate you, but I love you too damned much."

She could tell by the look on his face that it took a second for her words to register. When they did, he tugged her into his arms and wrapped them low around her back, surrounding her. She rested her head on his broad chest and clung to him. Fear and elation beat tattoos inside her, and her heart pounded in time with her surging emotions.

"Jess…Jess…Jess," he murmured. "I was sure I'd

lost you."

"Me too."

He held her as though he would never let her go. Kissing his cheek, she absorbed the reality of his presence into her pores, the long, harsh weeks draining away as they rocked together.

"Don't you get it?" She pushed at him until he moved just enough for their gazes to meet. "I wanted to love you, to have your back, and you have mine. I've gotten a chance to witness functioning families in this house. That's my goal—all I sought from you. My dream was to be by your side to help you in all ways a couple does. That's what a partner is for."

He jerked, his body spasming, and her spirits crashed.

"Partner?"

The single word sliced through her. She had misjudged—again. He might have said he loved her, but he wouldn't share his life with her. This had just been window dressing.

She tried to wrest herself away, but he held tight.

"Right. Got it. You love me, but I'm still not in your life for good. It's how it always is. I don't really blame you, just like I didn't blame Craig. Me, my baggage, my crazy parents, it's all too much to handle. Thanks for loving me, even if that isn't enough."

A myriad number of emotions played over his face, but she refused to have faith in them. She'd been hurt one too many times. She was done. They had been over for a long time, whatever he now said.

"Jess, shh, stop. You don't have any reason to believe yet, but hold on a second."

She stopped but remained stiff in his arms.

"I need to show you something that may help, but I have to let you go to do it. Don't move."

He released her, and Jess stayed rigid, picking at random threads on her shirt.

Kai pointed to the bag still slung across his body and fumbled the flap open. "I didn't have any right to hope, after I threw you away, that you would take me back. But in case you did, I…" He faltered and cleared his throat. "I don't care if you change your name. That's not important. But I… It would be my honor…" He stopped again.

Opening his hand, he revealed a diamond solitaire ring that caught the sun's rays and refracted into the room.

"It's pure and clean, like you. Like my love for you and yours for me. Jess, will you marry me? I want you to stand by my side and be my wife, my companion, my lover. Forever."

Jess threw herself into his arms. Kai was still clutching the jewelry. She started kissing his neck and cheeks, butterfly kisses on his skin.

He laughed, and his laugh was tinged with a heavy dose of relief. "Is that a yes?"

"Oh, that is without a doubt a yes."

"Then allow me to get this on you." He took the ring and slid it over her finger and then folded her hand in his. "When I think of what I could have given up," he murmured and then shuddered.

She put her arms around him and drew him close, rocking them together. His welcome arousal nudged her. He sighed and kissed her, his lips moving over hers.

"You better not ever try to let me go again."

"Not a chance. You and me, we're in this for life."

He brushed her hair with a gentle finger and traced a line of moisture down her cheek. "If your parents come for you, they come for me. We're a pair now."

"They could hurt your career, just like they went for mine."

He cupped her chin, and his smile was warm and inviting. "None of that matters. Careers come and go, but people don't. I am lost without you, Jessica Baker. They can post all the shit they want online, call you and me from every number in the world. You and I will fight them together, and when you get tired, I'll bolster you. Your brother isn't the sole person in your corner anymore. I'm here, and I'm not going anywhere. Not ever. I understand you will have to learn to trust me again over time, but I will give you whatever you need to trust in me, and us, again. In actions and not just words."

She started to say that everything was fine and she was over it, but stilled the sentences before she spoke them. Kai wasn't the only one who had work to do.

"That's fair. I believe you mean it." Jess held up her hand and examined the ring again. "It's perfect. Thank you, Kai. I love you with all my heart. I just hope that's enough."

"It always has been. I was the fool who almost took too long to realize it. We're together in every way, Jess. You and me."

Jess flung her arms around him, and Kai grunted as he embraced her. She pressed into him, the weeks of pain easing. His hair was silk against her skin, and he trembled as he held her tight.

Her phone rang, and she started before checking the number. "It's Rocky."

Kai's body moved, and she was puzzled until she

determined he was laughing.

"As I said, there are at least three people in your corner, and I would wager more if you let people in. That pit bull of a brother of yours is going to come out here if we don't go back to the main house. I would do no less in his position."

She recalled where the curtains had shifted and nodded. "I bet you're right. Rocky is going to take time to warm up, but he will. This will come as a shock. I didn't tell him about me and you, so you have a lot to prove."

"I'm up to the challenge." He swept her into his arms again and kissed her. "I'm willing to do whatever it takes. We will work through this together. All of it. The engagement can be as long or as short as you require. I will never take you for granted again. I promise."

"I'll hold you to that. If I don't, my relatives will be there to remind me." A thrill went through her at the idea that she had a family. Her brother's and the new one she would create with Kai. She stepped back and offered her hand to him.

He clasped it and kissed the back. "I'm glad of that. Let's go face them. I hope he doesn't have a shotgun."

She tossed her hair, the anxiety fading. Her engagement ring shone on her finger, catching the sun that was still rising in the sky. "I'll protect you."

His face was lit from within. "You will. You always have. I love you, Jessica Baker. Let's go face the music."

Her laugh bubbled up from the dissolving stone inside her. "Yes, let's. In more ways than one."

Together, they exited the guesthouse and headed across the lawn to those she loved and trusted—and into their shared future.

A word about the author...

Claire can't remember a time when writing wasn't part of her life. Growing up, she used to write stories with her friends. As a teenager she started out reading fantasy and science fiction, but her diet quickly changed to romance and happily-ever-after. A native of Massachusetts and cold weather, she left all that behind to move to the sun and fun of California, but has always lived no more than twenty miles from the ocean.

In college she studied acting with a minor in creative writing. In hindsight she should have flipped course studies. Before she was published, she sold books on eBay and discovered some of her favorite authors by sampling the goods.

While she's not a movie mogul or actor, she does work in the film industry with her office firmly situated in the 90210 district of Hollywood. Prone to break out into song, she is quick on her feet and just as quick with snappy dialogue. In addition to writing she does animal rescue, reads, and goes to movies. She loves to hear from fans, so feel free to drop her a line.

~*~

Find Claire Davon online at:
http://www.clairedavon.com

Thank you for purchasing
this publication of The Wild Rose Press, Inc.

For questions or more information
contact us at
info@thewildrosepress.com.

The Wild Rose Press, Inc.
www.thewildrosepress.com